UNfabulous!

The Perfect
Moment

PETER J. PALOMBI SCHOOL
LEARNING CENTER
133 McKinley Ave.
Lake Villa, IL 60046

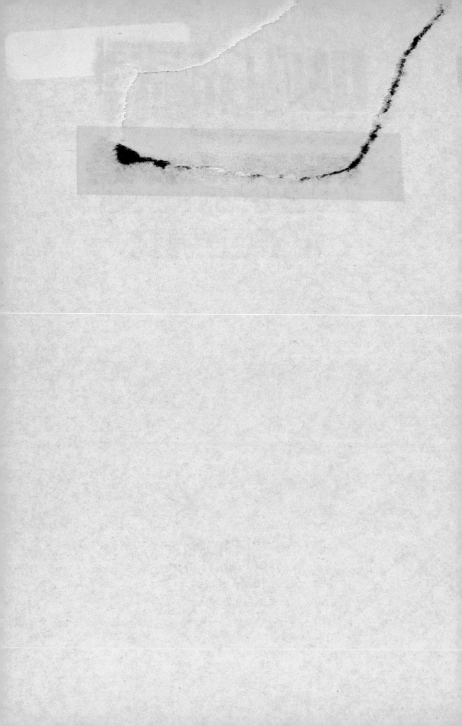

The Perfect
Moment

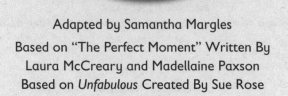

Adapted by Samantha Margles

Based on "The Perfect Moment" Written By
Laura McCreary and Madellaine Paxson
Based on *Unfabulous* Created By Sue Rose

SCHOLASTIC INC.

New York   Toronto   London   Auckland   Sydney
Mexico City   New Delhi   Hong Kong   Buenos Aires

If you purchased this book without a cover, you should be aware that this book is stolen property. It was reported as "unsold and destroyed" to the publisher, and neither the author nor the publisher has received any payment for this "stripped book."

No part of this work may be reproduced in whole or in part, stored in a retrieval system, or transmitted in any form or by any means, electronic, mechanical, photo-copying, recording, or otherwise, without written permission of the publisher. For information regarding permission, write to Scholastic Inc., Attention: Permissions Department, 557 Broadway, New York, NY 10012.

ISBN-13: 978-0-439-89340-4
ISBN-10: 0-439-89340-2

All songs and lyrics contained herein written by Jill Sobule.
© 2004 FEEL MY PAIN (ASCAP)/Administered by BUG/TUNES BY NICKELODEON INC. (ASCAP)
All Rights Reserved. Used by Permission.
"Unfabulous Theme Song" written by Jill Sobule

© 2007 Viacom International Inc. All Rights Reserved.
Nickelodeon, Unfabulous, and all related titles, logos, and characters are trademarks of Viacom International Inc.
(s06)

Published by Scholastic Inc.
SCHOLASTIC and associated logos are trademarks and/or registered trademarks of Scholastic Inc.

12 11 10 9 8 7 6 5 4 3 2

7 8 9 10 11/0

Printed in the U.S.A.
First printing, February 2007

The Perfect Moment

Summer. Have you ever noticed how it takes forever to arrive? It's the light at the end of the tunnel for the whole spring. It seems like it will never get here with all the tests to take and papers to write. There's homework to finish and chores to be done. And then, finally, school lets out, and summer's here.

Oh, summer. At long last — the season we've all been waiting for. There are long days, with sunlight that never seems to end. The nights are warm enough that you don't have to cover up your cute tank tops with sweaters. Without school, you can sleep in and forget about homework. The days are totally free and you have all the time in the world . . . to be miserable.

Yes. I was miserable.

You see, I finally got up the nerve on the last

day of school to tell Jake, the boy I've liked for as long as I can remember, how I really felt about him. Jake Behari — those dark eyes, the perfect hair, his irresistible smile, and, on top of all that, he's pretty much the nicest guy in school — and when I read what he wrote in my yearbook, I realized that he'd liked me, too. I mean he *like*-liked me.

I decided to go to his house that same day and tell him how I felt. I got there just in time — just in time to see Jake and his family drive away, on their way to Canada for the whole summer. And he still didn't know how I felt.

With summer here and no distractions, missing my chance with Jake was pretty much all I could think about. Every night I would sit alone in my room, staring at the ceiling. And the only thing that kept running through my head was: *How did I mess this up so completely?*

Then one night, Nancy came trotting through my door. Nancy's the greatest dog in the world, and I can always count on her to make me feel better. On this particular night she was holding something in her teeth when she came in.

"What is it, girl?" I asked her as I bent down to see

what she had in her mouth. It was an envelope. And in neat letters on the front it said: *To: Addie. From: Jake.*

"A letter from Jake?" Really?

Nancy just gave me one of her typical looks that seemed to say, "Duh."

I felt my stomach do a somersault. I couldn't believe it! Where could this letter have come from?

Wait a second. Who cares? I'd had a letter from Jake in my hand for almost fifteen seconds and I still hadn't opened it! What was I doing? I tore the envelope open and read the short note inside:

Addie, look out your window. . . .

I rushed to my open window, where the drapes were fluttering in the breeze. As I pulled open the curtains, my hair was gently blown away from my face as the air from outside brushed past me. And there, standing on a ladder he had propped against the house in order to climb up to see me — was Jake!

"Jake? What are you doing here?" I couldn't believe my eyes. He was supposed to be away for the whole vacation. I felt shocked and excited and a little nauseous, all at the same time. "I thought you were in Canada!"

"I couldn't stay away from you the whole summer," Jake said with desperation as he grabbed hold of my hands and looked deep into my eyes. "I rode a moose back to America, just to see you."

"You rode a moose?" Jake was so romantic! Most people might have caught a bus or hitched a ride. Even riding a horse would have been okay. But not Jake. He tamed a wild beast just to return home to see me — no matter how perilous the journey. "How dangerous!"

"I'd do anything to see you!" he said passionately as he finished climbing through the window and came to stand in front of me.

We looked longingly into each other's eyes. I always knew Jake and I belonged together, and this was the perfect way for us to declare our feelings! Jake started to lean in, his eyes started to close . . . he was going to kiss me! This was like a dream!

"These aren't cleats!"

Huh? Where was that angry voice coming from? This was my perfect moment with Jake, and there's no angry man in my perfect moment with Jake.

"Cleats! Cleats! Cleats!"

The funny thing about things that seem like they're out of a dream is that sometimes you're really dreaming.

Reality set in. I wasn't in my bedroom. I was at work. At my dad's store, Singer Sporting Goods. And in reality, there was an angry man waving a pair of sneakers in my face and yelling, "Cleats!"

"Um . . . I don't know if we have cleats." Okay. This *was* my job. But I only started working at my dad's sporting goods store so I'd have a little spending cash. It wasn't like it was my life. I didn't know everything we had for sale! Besides, what's wrong with just wearing sneakers?

"What kind of sporting goods store doesn't sell cleats?" Now the angry man was getting his angry wife involved.

"A bad kind, that's what!" angry man's angry wife chimed in.

"Thank you, Rebecca," angry man said with satisfaction and turned to raise his eyebrow accusingly at me.

As I looked around the store to see if someone might come to my rescue, I realized that the store was full of people yelling at other people and trying without

5

success to find whatever sporting goods they were looking for. People were waving socks, shorts, bathing suits, even fishing rods at whoever they could get to listen to them.

Where did all these angry people come from?

Just then, my dad came over from out of nowhere. He didn't look as though he'd even noticed the chaos in the store. Ignoring all the people who were yelling at him and wielding sporting goods with fury, he held a frilly purple nightie up to his chest as if he were trying it on and asked me, "Well? What do you think?"

I wasn't really sure what *I* thought, but it was pretty clear what Mr. and Mrs. Angry Cleats were thinking when Mr. Angry turned to his wife and said with exasperation, "Let's get out of here. This place is weird."

And with that, they pushed their way through the mob of furious customers and left.

Fortunately, I happened to know that my parents' wedding anniversary was coming up and that my dad wasn't really thinking of this negligee for himself. But still, frilly and purple?

I decided not to beat around the bush. "I don't think that Mom would really wear that."

Dad looked down at the nightie for a moment in thought and then shrugged. "Last year for our anniversary, I got her a blender. She didn't speak to me for two weeks. I'm going with the nightie." And with that, he turned around and headed back to the storage room. A whole lot of screaming customers swarmed around me and I was left with the disturbing image of my dad holding a purple lacy nightie against himself.

I wish school would start.

At least I didn't have to spend every minute of my summer working at Singer Sporting Goods for my dad. I did have enough time — and, thanks to my job, enough cash — to hang out with my best friends, Zach and Geena, at *Juice!*. The three of us had our drinks and were getting straws at the counter before finding a seat. We all had the afternoon free to meet up and we were now discussing my parents' anniversary.

"What? You're not getting them anything?" Zach, ever the sensitive guy, couldn't understand how anyone could skip an opportunity to do something nice for their parents. He stared at me in disbelief when I told him I didn't have a gift for them but his expression was kind of overshadowed by his new hairstyle.

Apparently, boys need to have a summer look

as much as girls do. I wasn't surprised when Geena refurbished her wardrobe for vacation. There was no way my stylish friend would be caught dead in last season's outdated looks, especially since she'd decided it was time to find a boyfriend. She made sure she was always ready to meet that special someone at any moment, and her outfits — which usually consisted of brightly colored tank tops, flirty skirts or short shorts, and strappy sandals — were carefully chosen to maximize her chances of catching the eye of her one and only.

Zach had decided to go au naturel for the summer. He'd taken out his dreads and opted to wear his hair in a slightly retro 'fro. I have to admit that it looked pretty cool, but it was taking me some time to get used to it.

"I sent them an e-card that had dancing bunnies on it and the message said 'Hoppy Anniversary,'" I said lamely in my defense.

"Hmm," Zach said, looking at me and nodding knowingly. "You can also get them a card with a little bird that says 'Cheap!'"

"Clever," I quipped back with a smirk. "Your brain must be as big as your hair."

Zach reached up and gave his hair a gentle pat

to see that it was in place. "It's my new summer 'do. I gotta be free," he said, looking wistfully off into the distance. Leave it to Zach the activist to make a social statement with his hair.

We made our way from the counter to an empty table by the door. *Juice!* was always bustling when there was no school, and we were lucky to find a table.

"*Vos grands cheveux sont très beaux,*" Geena cut in.

"What?" Zach said, giving her a confused look. He may be all about saving the world, but I guess Zach's not as *worldly* as Geena.

"She's learning French," I explained since Zach was still looking at Geena like her head had just spun all the way around on her neck. "She's decided to move to Paris since there are no boys here."

"This is my longest dry spell yet," Geena proclaimed with determination. "I figure it's time to try a new country."

That made me think about how *my* boy had left the country. "It worked for Jake," I lamented with a sigh.

"Just because Jake's in Canada doesn't mean he's found some new girl," Geena said pointedly. She wasn't going to let me wallow in self-pity and tried to tell me repeatedly that things could still work out for me and Jake.

Just then, the doors behind us burst open and in walked Maris, Cranberry, and the equally awful Patti Perez. As if Maris and Cranberry weren't bad enough on their own, Patti added a whole new dimension to their nasty group. The three of them were laughing and enjoying themselves as they entered the juice bar.

"You and Jake are back together again?" Maris was asking Patti as she grabbed her arm eagerly.

My heart stopped.

Patti nodded and smiled deviously. "He's in town for the weekend. We're going to his cousin's wedding together."

"That is *sooo* romantic!" Cranberry cut in as she came up on Patti's other side. The three of them giggled and, flipping their hair flamboyantly, they made their way over to the counter.

I couldn't move. I couldn't breathe. Could this possibly be true?

I turned to look over at the three of them. Patti turned slowly toward me. She gave me a knowing look full of fake sympathy and said, "Ooooh. That must make you feel . . . kind of like this —"

And I swear that at that moment a linebacker from the New York Jets came barreling through *Juice!* and slammed into me, pushing me and my chair across the floor and crushing me against the wall.

At least, that's what I felt like.

Actually, Patti never even acknowledged me. There was no football player and I was still sitting at the table with Geena and Zach. But my insides were demolished all the same.

"I can't believe it!" I had to shake my head to be sure this was real and looked back and forth between my two friends. "Jake and Patti?"

"Uh-oh," Geena said with a concerned look. "Why don't you try to get ahold of him again?"

"Again?"

Was she serious? I'd already told her all the ways I'd tried to get through to Jake.

First I took the easy route and e-mailed him. I figured he had to check his e-mail, even if he was in Canada. When he did, he'd just get back to me and things would be fine.

I'd finished writing a short and sweet note, telling

him that I needed to talk to him, and pushed SEND with confidence.

I was thrilled when I got a reply almost immediately. But my heart sank when I realized it was just an automated response:

Hey, it's Jake. I'm gone for the summer. Check ya in the fall.

P.S. Can someone tape Laguna Beach *for me?*

Apparently, Jake wasn't going to be e-mailing while he was in Canada.

Fine. I *knew* he didn't go to Canada without his cell phone. I wanted to be a bit more laid-back, but if calling was the only way to reach him, then I guess I would just have to call.

So, I'd swallowed my pride and dialed his number. And he even answered! I could just picture him at the top of some amazing Canadian mountain, dressed ruggedly for a hike, decked out with a backpack and hiking stick. But when he spoke, it was obvious that this mountain had terrible cell phone reception. I could barely hear him.

Hoping that if I yelled he'd be able to hear me, I screamed into my phone, "Hey, Jake! I hate to bother you while you're in Canada, but . . ."

He must have been having a hard time hearing

me, too, because the next thing I knew he interrupted me, sounding bewildered. "You . . . hate me?"

Just my luck that the only words I said that made it to Jake's ear in Canada were, *I, hate,* and *you.*

I panicked. "No! That's not what I said! I don't hate you!" But it was too late. He'd hung up. And can you blame him? He thought I called to say, "I hate you."

But hey, I'm a resourceful girl. I wasn't going to be stopped by my two thwarted attempts to contact Jake. For my next attempt I took out an ad in a Canadian newspaper that I figured he'd never be able to miss. I'd had a copy delivered to my house so I could see how it came out.

There it was, at the top of page one, for everyone to see. This was going to be perfect. Jake would see this and get in touch with me right away.

But what I read on the page *wasn't* what I'd asked them to write.

Dear Jake, Call me!!! But not on my cell. Eddie.

Eddie? You've got to be kidding me! I shook the paper as though *it* had been the one to mess up my name. "Addie!" I told it. "It's Addie!" But it was too late. It was no use. I was out of ideas.

I looked at Geena, frustrated just thinking about

all the ways I'd tried to get in touch with Jake. "The only thing I haven't tried is hitching a sled to Nancy and mushing all the way to Canada." I sighed deeply. "Do you know how to say 'my life is over' in French?"

"Don't freak out," Geena said comfortingly. "I'll ask around. Patti Perez and I have the same manicurist. Maybe *she* knows something."

"Enough with the overthinking." We can always count on Zach to be the practical one. "Look, Jake's in town. His cell phone will work. Just call him!"

I looked at my friends. They both nodded encouragement at me, so I reached into my bag for my phone. "I guess . . ." I said as I opened it and started to scroll through to his number.

Just then, Patti, Maris, and Cranberry took a seat at the table next to ours with their drinks. They were giggling maniacally and would totally have heard me on my phone. I couldn't call Jake now.

I looked at Zach and Geena as I closed my phone and put it away. "I'll call him tonight."

While all of my dreams about ending up happily ever after with Jake were being smashed to pieces, Ben, my older, cooler brother, was encountering his own romantic demons. Ben managed to score a job at *Juice!* a long time ago. He was great at his job and loved the attention he got from the girls who came in. At one point he'd been assigned to train a new employee, Jen, and the two of them ended up going out for a while. It didn't last very long (Nancy got jealous of Jen and made it clear that Ben would have to choose between them — Jen didn't take it very well when he chose Nancy) and ever since they'd broken up, Ben had been trying to find a way to win her back. At that particular moment, he was making yet another futile attempt to woo her.

"Okay, picture it," Ben began, painting a picture of romantic bliss starring him and Jen. "You, me, driving up the coast with the top down . . ." He had a starry look in his eyes as he described the scene.

"Driving?" Jen scoffed at him. You can't blame her for being skeptical. After all, Ben took his driving test about a hundred times and failed ninety-nine times. He started to freak out as the possibility of never getting a license began to loom larger and larger on the horizon. So, really, Jen's reaction was understandable. "You don't even have a —"

"Driver's license?" Ben interrupted as he whipped

his brand-new license out of his pocket and held it up for her to see. He *had* passed the test on the hundredth try. "Still warm from the oven. So how about it, trainee? Wanna go for a ride this weekend?" Ben was glowing with triumph as he waved his license in front of Jen.

"I'm not your trainee anymore. And we're not together anymore." Jen had to remind Ben of that a lot. He just didn't get how this girl could resist him! "Besides . . . I've got plans," she added coyly, looking over the counter at someone and waving.

Ben followed her eyes to see who could possibly have stolen his would-be girlfriend out from under him. What he saw did not make him happy: Kirk, who was built like a quarterback, with the face of a model and the charisma of a movie star. He was smiling and waving back at Jen.

Jen was obviously into this guy. Her eyes got all big and she tilted her head down at an angle to peek out from under her uniform cap as she asked, "Kirk, you want the usual?"

"Yeah. Thanks," Kirk replied jovially. He was polite, too!

Ben's jaw dropped for a moment, but he pulled

himself together and prepared to take on this Kirk dilemma. "You know his usual?" he asked Jen with a sneer.

Jen looked pleased with herself. She locked eyes with Ben and answered, "IronMaster. Extra protein." Then she turned to start making Kirk's drink.

Ben jumped between her and the blender and held up a hand. "No, no." He was using his most civilized tone of voice. He was totally being Mr. Nonchalant. "IronMaster is my specialty. Let me," he said as he took the protein powder out of Jen's hand.

"Okay," Jen said, giving Ben a funny look. But he had the good-guy act down — which makes sense for someone whose life revolves around people liking him — so Jen just started to work on something else. "Thanks."

Ben took a quick look around to be sure that no one was watching and then got to work on Kirk's drink. He put all the regular ingredients into the blender, but then, before blending, he grabbed a big, messy handful of dirt from the tray where the wheatgrass was growing. He casually dropped the dirt into the blender with the rest of the IronMaster and started mixing it all into protein mud.

But Ben didn't realize he was being watched when he added the dirt to the drink. He was caught totally off guard when Jen popped up at his side out of nowhere.

"What are you doing?" she asked suspiciously.

"Come on, Jen. You don't really want to be with 'Jerk,'" Ben crooned as he gestured to the model-like teenage hunk.

"Kirk," Jen corrected him. She did not sound amused. She also didn't seem to think Ben's special treatment of Kirk's smoothie was too funny. She grabbed the blender and glared at Ben.

Ben cocked his head to one side as if he were carefully considering what Jen had said before he shook his head and said, "I'm pretty sure it's 'Jerk.'"

"See, *this* is why it didn't work out with us," Jen shot back at him. "You're totally immature." And with that, she poured Ben's concoction into the sink. She paused for a moment, looking at the blender, then she pointedly looked back at Ben and forcefully threw the blender into the trash.

Just then, Mike, the manager, came from the back room to check what was going on and saw the blender in the trash. "Hey!" he yelled at Jen in a whiny voice. "Those blenders are expensive! Why did you throw it away?"

Jen looked at Mike, then glared angrily at Ben. "Ask *him*," she said, pointing at Ben for emphasis. Then she stormed away.

Mike got right up in Ben's face, his voice shrill with anger and confusion, and asked again, "Why did she throw it away?"

I don't know how Ben explained the blender in the trash can because I had my own problems to deal with. Later that night, I found myself having a staring contest with my cell phone. You know, they seem all happy and innocent, cell phones, with their colorful covers and upbeat ring tones. But just as often as a cell phone can make something good happen, they can bring the world crashing down on you. I knew I needed to call Jake and find out if he was really together with Patti or if there was a chance that things could work out for us, but I was terrified of what the answer might be. Don't they say that ignorance is bliss? Right now, blissful ignorance was sounding pretty good.

Who was I kidding? If anything was worse than

knowing for sure that Jake was back with Patti, it was having to *wonder* if Jake was back with Patti without knowing. I was feeling the furthest thing from blissful.

Nancy came into my room and found me facing down my sparkly pink cell phone. She barked at me, as if to tell me I was being ridiculous. Nancy knows me far too well.

"All right! All right," I told her. I guess Nancy was right — it would be better to end the mystery and find out where I stood with Jake. So, I grabbed my phone off the bed and dialed Jake's number.

It rang once. Then a second time. Then it rang a third time . . . maybe no one was going to answer. The suspense was driving me crazy! But then I heard it. "Hello?"

Only it was a girl's voice. I was confused at first since I knew I'd dialed the right number and it never occurred to me that anyone but Jake would answer.

"I'm s-sorry," I stuttered. "I was trying to reach —"

But the girl on the other end cut me off before I could finish. "Jake Behari?"

"Yeah." I was still confused. Why was a girl

answering Jake's phone? "Who is this?" I asked. But I didn't even need her to answer, because at that moment I recognized the voice and my heart froze.

"Addie," she said with a girly laugh, "it's me. Patti." I couldn't breathe. Not that it mattered since she just kept talking, anyway. "We're at Jake's cousin's rehearsal dinner. Together. Jake's busy, but I can give him a message if you want. . . ."

I hung up. There was nothing for me to say. I had my answer. At a rehearsal dinner? Together? It was worse than I thought, and I was speechless.

I was startled out of my shock when my phone rang suddenly. I was so surprised, I screamed and dropped it. It rang again. Could this possibly be Jake calling me back? Was he going to explain? Would he try to apologize?

I reached down, picked up my phone, and flipped it over to see who was calling. I don't know if I was relieved or even more disappointed when I saw that it was Geena calling, not Jake.

I flipped open my phone and got right to the point. "It's true," I told her. "Jake and Patti are back together."

"I know." Far be it for Geena to be behind on the

news. That girl could find out anything. "According to Tina at Nail Heaven, the wedding's being held tomorrow night in Chinatown." And as if that weren't enough: "She also told me that Patti's a lousy tipper." Actually, I'm not sure I'm too worried about that.

"Well, that's it. Maybe Jake and Patti should just get married while they're there. It's over for me." I mean, come on. How could I compete with a girl who already had Jake at the altar? Clearly there wasn't anything to do now but throw in the towel and think about joining a convent.

I guess Geena didn't have such a bleak view of the situation because the next words out of her mouth were: "Not necessarily." She paused dramatically as I waited for her to explain what she meant. Finally she added, "I have the address."

I could tell Geena was proud of herself for getting this tidbit out of her manicurist, but I wasn't sure how it was going to help me. "What am I supposed to do, show up at the wedding and tell Jake I like him in front of his girlfriend?" Was she serious?

"Yes."

Huh?

"Addie, if you don't go to that wedding and tell

24

Jake that you like him, you'll spend the rest of your life wondering what could have been."

Geena knows me better than anyone. And you know what? She was right. I'd already wasted the first part of my summer wishing I'd gotten to Jake before he left for Canada. Now, staring me in the face, I had a second chance to tell him how I felt. Was I really going to let it pass me by?

"Maybe you're right," I conceded. Did I have anything to lose?

Geena, knowing full well she'd convinced me to crash this wedding and confess my feelings for Jake, felt no need to prolong our conversation. *"Oui. au revoir."* And with that, she hung up.

There were so many things for me to think about. Could the boy I liked really want to be with Patti? And if he used to like me, could he possibly like me again? Was there any chance that going to find Jake at that wedding would be anything other than a disaster?

I knew there was only one way to stop my mind from racing. I reached over and grabbed my guitar from the side of my bed, started strumming, and just let the words flow out of me:

Jake's at a wedding — I hope it's not his.
I could sit at home and wonder, or I could take a
big risk. . . .
If I don't go, I'll never know.
Tomorrow night, gotta put up a fight!

And after that, I knew exactly what I needed to do.

I found Ben at the kitchen counter with his laptop open. He had an intense look on his face and the light coming from the screen gave him an eerie glow as he hunched over to look at the computer. I could tell that whatever he was doing was extremely important to him. He didn't even glance at me when I came into the room but just kept typing something into a search engine and checking out the hits that came up afterward.

I'd already asked him for what I needed, and since he seemed to be ignoring me, I almost repeated myself. But before I had the chance to start again, Ben cut me off.

"No," he said simply.

"But I really need to go! It's an emergency!" I hated having to beg Ben to help me, but there was no other option in this situation. I needed a ride to Chinatown. And as much as Geena and Zach could help me with the rest of the plan, that was something that neither one of them could do for me for a few years to come. I couldn't wait a few years for this.

"Chinatown is just a bunch of dirty alleys, seedy tattoo parlors, and strange people. Besides, I'm busy stalking Jen's new boyfriend." Throughout this, Ben never took his eyes off the computer.

Stalking her boyfriend? "That's creepy," I told him because, really, stalking a girl is bad enough. But when you stoop to stalking her boyfriend? That's the stuff scary movies start off with. But when I thought about it for a minute, I realized that stalking Jen's boyfriend made Ben kind of a weirdo. So, by his own description, he should be right at home in Chinatown.

"I've got to find out where he takes her," Ben tried to explain. "Whenever they turn around, I'll be there." Ben was sounding more obsessed by the second. "Aha!" Ben cried triumphantly at the laptop, catching me by surprise. "Mr. Kirk McKenzie, I see you have a speeding ticket on record! Let's see how Jen likes dating a criminal." He quickly started writing something down on a piece of paper and I realized there was no way I was going to convince Ben to give up his mission to uncover intelligence about Kirk. But I couldn't give up. Perhaps I could use this little obsession of Ben's to my advantage if I gave it some thought.

"Right," I said as I started to back out of the room. To be honest, Ben was freaking me out a little bit with this whole stalking thing. "Well, good luck with that." And I was out of there.

I spent Friday night figuring out how to get Ben to drive me to Chinatown so I could get to Jake and tell him how I felt about him. I knew I'd have to get to Ben through Jen, and I came up with a foolproof plan to make Ben *want* to go to Chinatown. Normally there's no way I'd be allowed to go to Chinatown, but my parents had chosen that night to celebrate their anniversary. They would be out all night doing . . . well, doing whatever it is that parents do on anniversaries. And what they didn't know about me and Chinatown wouldn't hurt them.

At *Juice!* the next day, I put my plan into action.

I got there early and started leaving flyers on all the tables. Then I found a seat at a table to wait and see if I would need to do more. When Kirk came in a little while later to get a drink and make a date with Jen, I knew I had him right where I wanted him.

Don't get me wrong, I actually think Kirk is kind of a nice guy. At least, I don't have anything against him. But I happened to know that he was what some might call "lacking" when it came to creativity. And since I had a feeling he'd be trying to come up with something to do with Jen on their date that night, I decided to help him out.

When he first sat down at the table, he put his muffin down on the flyer without even looking at it. I was worried. But when he picked the muffin up to take a bite, my fabulous flyer caught his attention. I could see his eyes taking in the words on the paper in front of him. PEKING ACROBATS the flyer said in big letters. It then went on to describe this amazing show that was taking place that night. And it just *happened* to be in Chinatown.

I figured a paper airplane flyer might help him make up his mind — so I sent one flying at his table. It hit him in the head. Oops. He turned to see where it had come from but I dropped the next flyer I had started folding and I don't think he knew I was the one who had targeted him. I gave him my best "who me?" look, and he seemed to lose interest.

I watched as Kirk got up from his table and made his way over to the counter where Jen was working. Ben was there, too, standing a few feet away, about to fill a cup with some iced tea from the dispenser. But when he saw Kirk talking to Jen, his attention strayed from the task in front of him and he focused on their exchange.

"What time are you off?" Kirk asked Jen as he leaned toward her over the counter.

"Six," Jen answered with a flirty smile. I could see Ben leaning in and trying to hear what they were saying.

"I heard the Peking Acrobats are in Chinatown tonight." Yes! He took the bait! "They're supposed to be amazing. . . . Do you want to go?"

"I'd love to," Jen answered warmly. This was almost *too* easy.

Ben had totally forgotten about the iced tea, which was now spilling all over the floor as his temper flared. The tea probably would have ended up all over the floor, anyway, since he threw the cup down in frustration when he heard Jen accept Kirk's offer.

*   *   *

When Ben got home later, I could hear him storming through the house.

"Addie!" he called out. Then he mumbled to himself, "I'll show Kirk."

I opened the door to my bedroom just enough to look at Ben in the hall. He had a crazed look in his eye and was breathing heavily.

"You still want to go to Chinatown?" he asked.

I just smiled at him and turned back to my room, where Geena and Zach had been waiting with me to see what happened.

"It worked," I told them, excitedly shutting the door. Geena and I bounced in celebration. Then again, did we ever really doubt that my genius master plan would work?

"Très magnifique," Geena declared.

Zach just shook his head at us. "What is it with you two? The mind games . . . the scheming . . ." He shuddered visibly before finishing with: ". . . the French?" Boys will never understand how girls' minds work. I guess some of us *do* have kind of roundabout ways of getting what we want.

Sure, it would have been easier to tell Jake how I

felt on the last day of school. But if I had, I would have missed the chance to trick my brother into driving me and my friends to a neighborhood where I'm not allowed to go on the night of a stranger's wedding so I could crash that wedding and *then* tell Jake how I felt about him in front of his whole family and his date.

Hmmm . . . maybe Zach had a point.

But none of that mattered now. Geena and I exchanged knowing smiles.

"We have to find the perfect thing for me to wear," I told Geena.

"Something with sparkles," Geena immediately added. This was going to be great.

"Hey," Zach said, interrupting our planning. "What about me?"

Geena gave him an appraising look and then shook her head. "You can't pull off sparkles," she told him flat out.

"No!" Zach whined. "I want to go to Chinatown."

"Really?" This came as a surprise to both Geena and me. Wasn't it about ten seconds ago that Zach told us he couldn't even understand why we would plan something like this? What could possibly make him so interested in getting involved in our devious scheming all of a sudden? I didn't get it, but he sounded really excited about going.

"Yeah," he enthused. A look of euphoria swept over his face as he went on. "Chinatown's a fantastic melting pot of history . . . culture . . . and tables full of ten socks for a dollar. There's no way I'm missing that!"

Of course. Why didn't I know Zach would want to come? He was right, Chinatown had it all: history, culture . . . and socks.

Like I said, my parents were going out that night. Now that I had my ride figured out and Geena had helped me pick out a sparkly outfit, the next part of my plan just involved seeing my parents out the door. Zach, Geena, Ben, and I were in the living room in front of the TV. We had our popcorn popped and a movie ready to go. Geena and I were cozied under a blanket that was pulled up under our chins, Zach was distractedly munching on popcorn, and Ben was stretched out in the easy chair.

It seemed like forever until Mom and Dad finally came down to say good-bye before heading out on their big anniversary date. It's so cute how grown-ups will get all dressed up sometimes. Mom had on a sweet red dress and Dad had gone so far as to put on a button-down shirt and slacks. And was that gel in his hair? You could tell they were excited to be going out for the evening.

"You sure you'll be okay?" Mom checked for the zillionth time. She never understood how any of us were able to get by for any period of time without her. "Safe? Warm? Dry? Fed? Bathed —"

"Mom," Ben cut in before she got to asking about anything embarrassing. His voice was cool, calm, and dripping with reassurance. "Please. Go. Enjoy your anniversary dinner."

"What can I say? I'm a mom. We worry even when our kids are just staying home watching a movie." She sounded kind of joking when she said it, but I've always wondered if moms didn't have some special sixth sense that alerted them when their kids were up to something and *that's* what made them worry about the movie watching. We all gave her our most innocent and good-hearted looks to let her know that there was really nothing for her to worry about.

"We'd better go," Dad said. "Reservations." You could tell he was impressed with himself for making plans to go to a restaurant that actually takes reservations, instead of his usual spur-of-the-moment trip to the Pancake Palace.

Mom gave us one more maternal look of concern and love before saying, "Bye," and walking out the door with Dad.

The four of us kept those perfect-child looks plastered on our faces as they left the house. We watched through the window as they got into the car and, just in case, we stayed that way until the car was down the road and out of sight.

But as soon as they were really gone, we were ready.

Geena and I threw back the blanket, revealing our carefully selected wedding-crashing outfits. I'd totally succeeded with the sparkles plan and found an amazing hot-pink dress that sparkled like a jewel. I have to say, I looked pretty fabulous in that dress. Geena's outfit was less eye-catching since, as the best best friend in the world, she wanted me to be the one in the spotlight on my big night. But Geena looks fantastic all the time, anyway.

Ben hopped up and grabbed the phone. "I'm forwarding the house phone to my cell," he said as he dialed a series of numbers. Ben was no stranger to this type of deceptive maneuvering. He was going to be good for more than just the ride to Chinatown, that was obvious.

"We're going to get in the car," I told Ben as Geena, Zach, and I headed for the door.

Ben finished rigging the phone and was digging frantically through a drawer of keys when he suddenly froze. "Wait!"

We stopped and looked at him even though we were halfway out the door already.

"What?" I demanded. This wasn't the time to be slowing things down. We had a wedding to crash!

"They left Mom's car. I can't drive stick." Ben looked crestfallen and defeated.

You see, Ben had really wanted to learn stick so he could drive any car at all. But Dad had been designated by Mom to be Ben's driving coach, and the problem was that *Dad* didn't know how to drive stick. He'd even taken lessons to try to learn so he could teach Ben and, probably more important, so he wouldn't have to admit to his son that he couldn't. But his efforts to learn were fruitless. To this day, Ben still hadn't figured out how to get a standard transmission to work for him. It looked like our plan was thwarted before we even got out the front door.

"*I* can drive stick," Geena said proudly as she grabbed the keys out of Ben's hand.

Geena? Geena can drive a stick shift? Geena, who spends as much time choosing her nail polish as she does on her homework, knows how to drive? And not only does she know how to drive but she can drive stick? Needless to say, the rest of us were stunned. Geena explained it to us.

"My dad always lets me practice in the church parking lot. In case of emergencies."

Was there any question that this was an emergency?

"You don't have a license," Ben pointed out, grabbing back the keys. Ah, yes. There was that one little problem. Leave it to Ben to stifle my last ray of hope.

"I'll just tell you what to do," Geena suggested.

"You know, Ben," Zach said, "she's good at that." It's true. If there's one thing Geena knows almost as well as fashion, it's telling people what to do.

And that's how we ended up in my mom's car on our way to Chinatown.

Geena made it sound like telling Ben how to drive stick was going to be easy, but there's a reason he hadn't learned how to do it on his own yet. It was hard. Since I don't even know how to drive an automatic car, I can't really tell you what it was Ben did wrong, but Geena kept telling him to put one foot down and then the other, to "ease up on the clutch" and "give it a little gas," but the only thing Ben was able to get the car to do was lurch over and over again as we inched down the street. The engine kept making these awful revving noises and whenever Ben tried to shift, there was an earsplitting sound of metal grinding on metal.

Ben was freaking out and clutching the steering wheel like his life depended on it. I had a firm grip on the armrest as I focused on my motivation for being in this car: Jake. I had to get to Jake. Zach was sitting quietly in the backseat as his face got greener and greener with each lurch of the car. And Geena was trying desperately to get Ben to follow her directions.

"Ben," Geena insisted. "You have to shift."

Ben gave up trying to shift a while ago when he couldn't take the sound of grinding metal anymore. It had helped make the ride less noisy, but it didn't seem like we were going to be able to break ten miles an hour. At least we wouldn't get stopped for speeding.

"No. I feel good like this," Ben said unconvincingly. I'm not sure if it was the fact that every single muscle in Ben's body was visibly tense or the pained expression on his face that gave him away, but it was clear Ben did not feel good.

"You can't drive all the way to Chinatown in first gear," Geena tried to explain for, like, the tenth time. "It's bad for the engine."

"We're moving, aren't we?" Ben yelled back at her.

So Geena gave up trying to give Ben instructions on how to drive and we lurched onward for what felt like forever. She must have been right, though, about driving in first being bad for the engine, because after a while the car just stopped working.

"Why are we stopping?" I had the horrible feeling that I knew why, but I needed to ask.

"Because your brother fried the engine," Geena said, giving Ben her best "I told you so" look. "We're stuck."

I felt the scream building inside me. It started deep in my stomach and worked its way into my throat and out of my mouth at an ear-piercing decibel. Stuck?

We couldn't be stuck. Not after everything. Not after I devised the perfect plan that even involved getting *Kirk* to Chinatown. I had one chance to get to Jake and this was it! If I missed it, he'd be together with Patti and on his way back to Canada and I'd never know if I stood a chance of being with him. There was absolutely no *way* we could possibly be stuck after we'd come so far!

I was still screaming!

As I finally felt the last bit of scream empty out of my chest, I noticed that everyone else in the car had their hands over their ears and a pained expression on their faces. *Oops.*

"Are you done?" Zach asked cautiously as he peeled one hand away from his ear.

"You guys don't understand. I have to get to that wedding!" Didn't they get it? My future happiness was riding on whether or not I could get to that wedding in time to win Jake back.

"Addie," Geena said, grabbing hold of me by the arm. "It's okay. We just have to wait for the engine to cool down."

Wait, you mean we weren't totally stuck? "How long will that take?" There was hope!

Geena kind of turned away and mumbled her answer but I still heard her loud and clear. "Four to six hours."

I felt another scream start building inside my chest. I opened my mouth to let it out, but before the sound escaped my lips, Ben reached over and touched my arm.

"Addie, look," he said, pointing out the window. "We're here."

And we were.

The four of us climbed out of the car to find that we were standing in front of a big iron gate covered in ornate Chinese characters and dragon heads. On the sidewalk on either side of the gate were stone sculptures of life-size lions, like they were standing guard at a magical kingdom.

And what we saw when we passed that gate looked like a magical kingdom. Red paper lanterns with black Chinese letters emblazoned on them were hanging everywhere. Neon signs on every store declared things I can only imagine (they were all in Chinese). People filled the streets because there were hardly any cars. Rickshaws — people on bikes pulling passengers in little carriages behind them — drove by every few seconds. The store windows were filled with food: bakeries had breads, cookies, and pastries, and restaurants had everything from live fish in tanks to roasted ducks hanging by their feet on display. The sidewalks were crowded with booths and tents where people were selling everything from bamboo plants to jade figurines. It was like we'd entered another world.

All of us were riveted by what we saw. It had a kind of hypnotic effect with all the lights and the people milling about.

"Anybody know where we're going?" Zach asked.

"I've got the address," I said as I dug into my bag to look for the piece of paper Geena's manicurist had written it down on. I pulled it out, read it, and then looked around at the street signs to figure out where we were. Then I realized we had another problem.

"None of the street signs are in English," I said, looking frantically from one cryptic sign to another. Why couldn't something about this trip be simple?

Just then a horn honked and a rickshaw pulled up alongside us. A guy who might have been in his twenties was riding the bike that pulled the carriage. He seemed to be dressed comfortably in baggy pants and his loose-fitting red T-shirt that said RICKY RICKSHAW on it in black script.

"Hey, y'all," he said to us energetically. "Ricky Ricky-Rick-Rick-Rickshaw at your service. Need a lift?" Our knight in shining . . . rickshaw? Whatever.

"Totally!" I wasn't passing up this chance to find Jake. "Thank you so much."

I started to climb into the carriage and the others were right behind me. But before we could all get in, Ricky looked us over and then held out a hand to stop us.

"Whoa. I can't take four people. Ricky Rickshaw can only take three." Now that I stopped to look at it, the carriage was pretty small. And I guess the guy *was* pulling it on a bicycle. But Geena and I were little and even if Zach's hair was big, I was sure it didn't weigh much!

"Perfect," Ben said, pushing us out of the way and climbing into the rickshaw. "Take me to the Peking Acrobats."

"Ben! What are you doing?" I tried to grab hold of his arm but Ben just brushed me off. Was he really going to leave us here?

"You heard the man," Ben said defensively. "He can't take four." He turned to the man on the bicycle. "Hit it, Ricky." And with that, Ricky rickshawed my brother into the night, leaving the three of us stranded on the sidewalk.

Geena sighed and looked sadly at her feet. She was wearing a new pair of strappy, high-heeled sandals that were clearly not cut out for hoofing it through Chinatown. "I guess we're still walking," she lamented.

Zach quickly jumped behind Geena and me and gestured for us to lead the way. "Good, you guys walk ahead in case there are any puddles or sticky spots." Ah, yes. Zach, always the gentleman. Geena and I both gave him a look. "I'm not taking any chances with these babies," Zach explained, pointing out his new pair of flashy red-and-white sneakers. "I've been saving for these for months. Cruelty-free sneakers aren't cheap, you know."

Making the girls walk ahead seemed pretty cruel to me, but whatever.

Geena, Zach, and I walked around for a while, trying to figure out where we were going. I tried to ask a few people for directions, but no one was able to help us find the wedding. We stopped to rethink our plan in front of a restaurant window with a bright sign and a big tank on display.

"Hey, look," I said, pointing out the restaurant's sign. "The original Hong Kong Palace." Geena was unimpressed, but Zach took one look at that window and seemed like he'd been caught on a fishing line and was being reeled into it. I realized what he was looking at was in the display tank.

"Lobster!" Zach declared with desire painted across his face. There was only one lobster left, alone in its tank in the window, and I guess Zach's heart was set on having it.

"Zach! There'll be food at the wedding," I told him as I tried to pull him away.

"No! I have to free that lobster!" Zach was looking frantic and determined.

"What?" This was a bit much, even for my animal-loving, cause-fighting friend. "You're kidding, right?"

Zach tore his eyes away from the lobster for a moment and turned to face me. He put his hands on my shoulders, looked me dead in the eye, and said, "Addie, I see it now. I was destined to come here. Not just to find ten socks for a dollar but to save that lobster."

"Zach, we have a wedding to find," I cried, hoping I could dissuade him from this crustacean crusade.

"No, Addie." Zach looked serious. "*You* have a wedding to find. *I* have a lobster to save." And with that, he disappeared into the original Hong Kong Palace.

I was stunned. We'd come to Chinatown to do one thing — find Jake. Now I'd lost my brother and the rickshaw to the Peking Acrobats, and Zach was on a mission to liberate seafood.

"I can't believe this. Geena, you're not going to

ditch me, too, right?" I asked, turning to Geena for reassurance.

But Geena was gone.

Wait, Geena was gone, too? How do these things happen to me? Best friends are the people you're supposed to be able to count on, especially during emergency missions to crash other people's weddings!

"Geena?" I called down the street.

Nothing. All I saw were the same Chinatown tourists, tables of knickknacks, and tents of items for sale.

Then I saw something that caught my eye. There was a tent off to one side that had a slightly more exotic look to it. Pinned to the tarp that was hanging over the entrance was a big sign that said FORTUNE-TELLING. I had a hunch this was just the kind of place that would have caught Geena's attention, too.

I pushed the tarp covering the entrance to one side and stepped into the tent. The inside was dimly lit by candles that were spread throughout the space. There were crystals and jars of herbs scattered around the edge of the room and in the center was a table. At the table sat a Chinese woman who had a deck of strange-looking cards laid out in front of her. Across from her, with her back to the door, was Geena.

She was giving the fortune-teller her undivided attention.

"I see this year your soil and fire are much stronger than your wood and water," the fortune-teller was saying while she waved her hands enigmatically in front of her face.

"Which means . . . ?" Geena asked.

"Good luck," the fortune-teller responded with a nod and a hint of satisfaction.

I came up alongside Geena in time to see her smile happily at this. She looked up at me in surprise when she realized I was looking over her shoulder.

"Oh. Hi, Addie." It was as if she hadn't just abandoned me outside on the sidewalk moments ago. "I just wanted to see if my boy slump would be over soon."

It seemed like everyone was trying to get something out of this trip to Chinatown.

"It will definitely be over," the fortune-teller declared emphatically. Geena was looking more pleased by the second. Then the fortune-teller added, "In Cincinnati."

Geena stopped looking happy. I guess Cincinnati wasn't exactly her idea of the ideal place for a romantic rendezvous.

"Cincinnati? What about Paris?" Geena stood up in anger and was giving the fortune-teller a menacing look. It looked like Geena's French lessons weren't going to be put to good use.

"We have to go," I said, trying to pull Geena out of the tent. That's when the fortune-teller looked at me.

"Ahh, you, too, are looking for something," she told me. Wait. Was it possible this lady was for real? How could she know that?

"Yeah. I'm looking for a wedding." Maybe she could tell me where this stupid wedding was. I dug out the piece of paper with the address on it and tried to show it to her. "Do you know where this is?"

She didn't even look at the paper in my hand. In fact, just then, she kind of twitched a little and her eyes seemed to glaze over. It reminded me of some creepy movie. When she spoke, her voice sounded different than it had before, kind of lower and gravelly.

"What you seek cannot be found where you are searching," she said in this weird voice.

"What?" I asked her.

"The bells will lead you to your heart's desire." Okay. This lady was wacko.

"Right. The bells," I said as I nodded and started

taking slow steps backward toward the door of the tent. "Gotta go!" And with that, I bolted out of the tent, pulling Geena behind me.

The fortune-teller was yelling after us in Chinese when we ran out so we didn't stop to catch our breath until we got a little way down the street.

"Well, that was a big waste of time," Geena declared. I knew that she was thinking more about the information regarding her dry spell ending in Cincinnati than finding the wedding, but she was right either way.

I was running out of time so I strengthened my resolve once more. "Someone around here has to know where this place is."

We were about to start our search again, when we heard voices coming out of an alley.

"Run, Jet Li! Run like the wind!!!"

Okay. This was Chinatown, but it seemed unlikely that a famous action-movie star was hanging out in a random alley. Geena and I looked at each other and shrugged before we started following the voices.

We rounded the corner into an alley and saw several old men dressed in straw hats and buttoned-up sweaters, gathered around some sort of tiny racetrack. It was made of wooden boards separated by about a foot and closed off with another board at each end. The lanes it made were about six feet long. Four men were just looking on with interest but two of them were jumping up and down, money in hand, and yelling at whatever was in the lanes.

"Get the lead out, turtle!" one of the jumping men cried at the lanes.

Turtle? Geena and I got a little closer and peered into the lanes. Sure enough, there were two turtles, each with a number painted on its back, making their way slowly and calmly from one end of the lanes to the red line at the other end.

Finally, turtle number two crossed the red line. One of the men stopped shouting immediately and slumped over in disappointment. I guess he was the loser. The other man was still jumping up and down.

"Ha-ha! Pay up, loser," the owner of the winning turtle demanded of the slumped man, who handed over the money he held in his hand. Then his head shot up and his eyes focused on me.

"Go away from here," he yelled, pointing at me. The other men all turned to look at me and Geena. "You're bad luck!"

"No she's not," Geena declared, coming to my

rescue. "Her soil and fire are very strong this year."
This seemed to impress the guy. I guess the fortune-
teller wasn't a total waste of time after all.

"Oh," he said more calmly. "What do you want?"

Here goes nothing.

I held out the paper with the address on it one
more time. The turtle guy took the paper and looked at
it for a moment before he started nodding.

"Oh, yeah," he said with confidence, still nodding.
"Not far." He hesitated for another second and seemed
to consider the situation. Then he picked up his losing
turtle and held it over to me. "I'll tell you if you kiss Jet
Li for luck."

Stupid fortune-teller.

It didn't seem like I had a whole lot of choice at
this point. So, while Jet Li came closer and closer, I closed
my eyes, puckered up, and got ready to plant a smooch
on his little turtle head.

The Peking Acrobats were performing not far from where all of this was happening to Geena and me. A couple of acrobats had been placed outside the theater to attract a crowd, and a barker was there to usher people inside once they stopped to check out the demonstration. One of the acrobats was contorting her body into all sorts of unbelievable shapes, while the other had two poles, each with branches like a tree, and on each branch was a spinning plate. You know—typical Saturday-night stuff.

"Come inside if you want to see the amazing Peking Acrobats! Like this," cried the barker, gesturing behind him to the pretzel-shaped woman and plate-spinning man. "Only better!"

Jen and Kirk had already arrived and were standing in front of the theater, watching the acrobats do their tricks.

"These guys are amazing," Jen proclaimed, her eyes wide as the woman stayed in her pretzel shape and lifted her entire body off the ground with her hands.

"I haven't even noticed. I can't stop looking at you," Kirk said dreamily to Jen. She swatted at him playfully but she was clearly into his corny come-ons.

Kirk wasn't the only person at *Juice!* who'd seen the flyers since I'd put them everywhere. And just in case some of my other friends were interested, I'd hit them with the idea, too. Literally.

"This is so cool. . . ." That was Mary Ferry. She's a great girl I know who goes out with another friend of mine, Duane. I'd happened to target Duane with a paper airplane flyer that afternoon. "I'm glad you thought of it," Mary said happily to Duane as she checked out the plate spinner.

"What are you talking about?" Duane asked her. "Addie threw this flyer airplane at us," he said, holding out the flyer to her.

Jen, however, was busy watching the acrobats and didn't hear him, which was probably just as well.

Suddenly the sound of a rickshaw bell rang out.

Just then, Ricky Rickshaw pulled up in front of the theater with his bell ringing loudly and screeched to a halt. Lots of people turned to look, including Jen. When she spotted Ben in the back of the rickshaw, a horrified look crossed her face.

"We have to get out of here. Now," Jen said frantically, pulling on Kirk's sleeve and looking all around.

"Why?" Kirk asked, totally bewildered.

But they were too late.

Ben immediately spotted Jen and Kirk and didn't even stop to count out the money for the fare. He just handed Ricky a wad of cash as he climbed out of the carriage.

"Thanks," Ben said offhandedly as he zeroed in on Jen.

"Ricky Rickshaw thanks *you*," Ricky said excitedly when he saw how much money Ben had handed him. Then he pedaled out of there with a big smile on his face.

Jen hadn't moved a muscle during Ben's entrance, but now she turned back to Kirk and gestured meaningfully over to where Ben was approaching. *"That's* why," she said angrily.

Ben put on his best confident swagger and strutted right up to Jen and her date.

"Jen! And Jerk! What a coincidence. I love acrobats, too. In fact, I can do a little hand-walking myself."

"Don't care," Jen said as she looked away. She tried to leave, but when she started to turn to walk off, Ben threw his feet in the air and began walking around on his hands right in front of her.

"Quit it, Ben," Jen cried, clearly unamused. Instead of convincing Ben to stop drawing attention to himself, Jen's cry had interested some of the people who had been watching the acrobats. When they saw Ben in his handstand, they shifted their attention and started moving over to where Jen and Kirk were standing.

Kirk put a hand on Jen's arm to calm her. "Let me handle this," he said soothingly. Then he tried to lead Jen around Ben and into the theater, but Ben just kept repositioning so that Kirk kept coming face-to-face with Ben's feet. (Or would that be face-to-*feet* with Ben's feet?)

"Excuse me," the barker was calling to the crowd, whose attention had been completely lost by the acrobats.

"Real acrobats over here! From Peking!" But despite his pleas, the crowd was riveted by Ben.

Finally, Kirk had had enough of Ben's feet in his face. With one swipe of his arm, he knocked Ben out of his handstand and onto the ground.

But Ben was not to be stopped. He popped right back up onto his feet and got face-to-face — for real — with Kirk. "I know about your criminal past, McKenzie," Ben said threateningly. Then he turned to Jen. "You're just lucky I warned you in time."

Ben obviously thought he had Kirk right where he wanted him. He took a step closer to him and pointed a finger in his face. "You're a real —"

That was all Ben could say before Kirk grabbed his wrist and twisted it, forcing Ben to spin awkwardly around so his back was to Kirk. Then Kirk pinned Ben's arm behind his back. The whole thing happened in a second and while Ben was wincing in pain — probably pain to both his arm and his pride — Kirk made the move look easy.

"Real what?" Kirk asked calmly over Ben's shoulder. "A real black belt in karate?" Wow. I think Jen might have really scored big with this Kirk guy. Cute, polite, *and* a karate master? I'm not sure I can blame her for picking him over Ben. . . . is that okay?

By now the crowd had lost all interest in the acrobats and had gathered in a circle around Ben, Kirk, and Jen. It sounded like people were starting to choose sides in the battle between Ben and Kirk, and voices kept popping out of the din, yelling support to one of them or an insult at the other. It was starting to look like a real-life episode of *Jerry Springer,* except there was no host egging them on and it was clear the barker was hoping this would stop as soon as possible. The poor barker was doing his best to get the crowd's attention back, but he wasn't having any success. He was starting to look concerned about the confrontation that was taking place.

"Stop!" the barker yelled at Kirk. "No fighting at acrobat show!"

Kirk let Ben go, but then Ben stumbled backward, out of Kirk's grip, and bumped into the acrobats, who had been trying to keep up their act the whole time. The contortionist had been balancing on her hands, but when Ben knocked into her, her hands collapsed from under her and she landed on her face in a puddle. The plate spinner had succeeded in keeping his focus through all of the madness, but when Ben backed away from the now-furious woman lying in a knot in a puddle, he ended up walking right into the other acrobat and caused all of his plates to spin out of control and off of their sticks. Most of the plates just fell to the ground and broke, but a few of them had enough momentum to go flying off in different directions and hit some of the people in the crowd who were getting caught up in the brewing mess.

"Ow," said one guy as he took a plate to the head. "Who threw a plate at me?" This just wasn't the acrobats' night, because the spinner had started to pick up his plates and when the man turned and saw him with the dishes in his hand, he decided that this must be his assailant. "Oh, it was you!" he cried as he charged the poor acrobat and gave him a good shove.

All around, the crowd was breaking into a panic. Some people were yelling; others were chasing after people they thought had tried to hurt them. Some people, like Mary and Duane, were just trying to get out of there before they got hurt.

"Run for it, Mary!" Duane cried, grabbing Mary's hand and pulling her out of the crowd.

Jen, on the other hand, stayed put, glaring at Ben. She didn't look happy about his attempt to "save" her from her derelict boyfriend. And even though most people would have realized by now that Ben's plan to win Jen back was a lost cause, the Singers don't give up easily and Ben wasn't done fighting. Considering my own desperate plot to find Jake, could I really blame him?

"I told you Kirk was a thug," Ben said triumphantly to Jen, who was looking angrier by the second.

"You are *so* immature," was all Jen said, shaking her head. She turned to walk away, but she stopped and said to Ben over her shoulder, "Do everyone a favor and grow up." Then she stormed off, leaving Ben and Kirk standing alone in the middle of the mob that had formed outside the Peking Acrobat theater.

Ben was riled up now and shouted after her, "You want to see mature? I'll show you mature." Then he stormed off in the opposite direction.

Kirk was standing alone now, looking kind of bewildered. His date had left him and people all around were fighting with one another.

I guess it shouldn't come as a surprise that someone called the police. A squad car pulled up right in front of Kirk, sirens blazing, and two cops jumped out.

"Police! Hands up!"

Looks like Kirk's night wasn't over after all.

Fortunately for me, kissing Jet Li had paid off. The man explained how to get to the address on my piece of paper and I finally found the restaurant where Jake's cousin was getting married. I couldn't believe I was finally there — I felt kind of like Dorothy arriving at Oz. Hey, I was even wearing ruby slippers! Okay, they were pink, not red. But close enough!

"This is the place," I said anxiously to Geena. My heart was pounding in my throat. Was I really about to crash a wedding and declare my feelings for Jake?

Yup.

"How do I look?"

Geena gave me an appraising once-over and then nodded knowingly. "Perfect," she assured me.

We climbed the steps, pushed open the door, and walked inside.

Trying to look casual, like we were just a couple of guests who were arriving late, we made our way into the impressive gathering. Geena and I were both caught off guard by the decor and the number of people. The place was packed!

I don't know if I've mentioned it before, but Jake's family is Indian. And they have a really big family. There were hundreds of people milling about in this building and they were all part of the wedding. The rooms were decked out with traditional Indian decorations, which are really colorful and interesting. Lots of the women were wearing saris, which, in case you don't know (and I have to say that I didn't until that night), are these beautiful outfits made of colorful fabric draped carefully around a woman's body and shoulders.

"This is definitely the place," Geena said, looking around.

The crowd was buzzing and the color of the clothes and the decorations were totally awesome. In addition to the guests, there were a bunch of servers walking around with trays of traditional Indian appetizers. The smell of the food was amazing. I was definitely ready for a snack, but I decided I should get started trying to find Jake. With all these people, who knew how long it would take to find him?

"I'm gonna go do a lap," I told Geena, then headed off. I knew I didn't have to worry about leaving Geena on her own. She never had a hard time fitting in at a party.

Turns out Geena wasn't alone for long. One of the servers came up to her the second I left. "Would you like an appetizer?" he asked her.

Geena looked up to say thanks and that was all it took—the girl was hooked.

This waiter was almost as cute as Jake. Almost. He was tall and had dirty-blond hair that fell down around his face. He had that healthy glow you get from being out in the sun, and his eyes were an amazingly deep shade of blue — and they were locked on Geena. I don't know whose fault it was, but as Geena walked toward him with a gleam in her eye and reached for a vegetable samosa on his tray, the tray went crashing to the floor. Banana fritters and naan went everywhere.

"Oh, man . . ." the waiter grumbled as he bent down and starting picking the fried fare up off the floor.

Everyone around stopped talking and turned to look when they heard the tray crash to the floor. "Real slick, Nate," he said to himself as he gathered up the spilled food.

With some guys, Geena would have been completely turned off by such a clumsy move. I mean, could she really risk being around someone who might endanger her fabulous outfits with their klutziness? That's how I knew that she'd really been struck with Cupid's arrow, because instead of smiling apologetically at him and taking the chance to disappear into the crowd while he picked things up, she actually bent down next to him to help.

"It could happen to anyone," she told him quietly with a warm smile. "Once, my skirt got sucked down an airplane toilet. While I was still wearing it."

"Really?" he asked her with a laugh. He was starting to look less upset.

"Talk about embarrassing," Geena went on. "I had to wear paper towels around my waist all the way to Albuquerque. And if you ever tell anyone that, I'll kill you," she added sweetly. Wow. Geena really must have been hit hard to volunteer *that* story.

*   *   *

On the other side of the banquet hall, I was making my way through the crowd and searching for Jake. I saw a staircase and climbed up it to get a better look. Once I got up there, I spotted Jake standing at the other end of the room. He was looking cuter than ever, all dressed up for the wedding. His shaggy hair was a bit more groomed than usual and he was wearing a tux. Can you say *amazing*?

He looked perfect standing there, all dapper and suave. Now was my chance.

"Jake!" I called across the room. "Jake!" I started to make my way down the stairs and over to where he was standing, but there were so many people I could barely move. I kept calling out his name, and I think I saw him looking over at me, but the crowd must have gotten in the way because we never made eye contact.

What I didn't realize at the time is that Jake hadn't been standing there alone. He was being carefully guarded by Patti Perez. She hadn't let him out of her sight all night. And while Jake wasn't sure if he'd really heard his name being called through the crowd, Patti *did* hear it. She also saw me coming.

She wasn't about to give me the chance to break

up her dream date with Jake, so she quickly thought of a way to keep him away from me. She grabbed him by the arm and started walking with him as fast as she could—in the other direction.

"Jake," Patti said, sounding as innocent as she could, which, considering who we're talking about, was impressively innocent. "Your cousin is looking for you. . . . She needs your help with some . . . Indian-wedding thing." Real smooth, Patti.

Poor Jake. He's too nice to even suspect that Patti would be lying to him. "Oh. Okay," he said, even though he was still looking back over his shoulder in the direction of where he'd heard my voice calling his name and maybe even seen me pushing my way through the crowd. "Did you see Addie here?" he asked Patti.

"No. Of course not," Patti answered with a smile and a shrug. Was she for real? Then I guess something else occurred to her because the next thing she said was, "Can I borrow your cell phone? I left mine at home."

"Yeah. Sure," Jake said as he took his phone out of his pocket and handed it to her. And then poor, unsuspecting Jake went to go find his cousin in some other part of the building.

"Thanks," Patti said. And as soon as Jake was gone,

her sweet smile turned to a devious grin as she casually dropped Jake's cell phone in the closest trash can.

At the time, I didn't know any of this had happened. All I knew was that I'd spotted Jake but that he didn't seem to be hearing me as I called out his name and tried to reach him. And before I could make my way through the crowd, Jake had disappeared.

A lot of things were happening at the same time at this point in the night. I'll try to tell you everything, but stop me if you get confused.

When Ben stormed away from the Peking Acrobats theater he had one thing on his mind: He was going to prove to Jen just how grown-up he really was. And to Ben, one thing declared adulthood more than anything else: tattoos.

It didn't take him long to find a tattoo parlor in Chinatown. *Tattoo* seemed like it was the only word on any of the buildings that wasn't in Chinese. But I don't think he would have misunderstood the huge neon sign above the parlor, anyway, given all the photos in the window of people who had gotten tattoos there.

"Oh, yeah," Ben declared with manly confidence

as he eyed a few of the images in the window and strutted into the shop.

I don't know if you've ever been to a tattoo parlor, but I think this was the kind that most people would avoid. It was dimly lit and the guy working there looked scruffy and dirty. I guess Ben couldn't have known any better since he was still two years away from being able to legally get a tattoo, but he was so caught up in his moment of grown-up glory, I don't think he even noticed.

Meanwhile, back at the Hong Kong Palace, Zach was gazing lovingly through the wall of a glass tank at his new friend, the lobster. He wanted the lobster to know that it was no longer pot-bound, so he whispered soothing words through the glass of the tank.

"Don't worry, little guy...." He paused as a thoughtful look crossed his face before adding, "Or girl. I don't mean to presume."

As he continued to watch the shellfish amble around the tank, Zach realized he could see the people having dinner on the other side. When he got a good look at the people there, he froze. Even though the water in the tank gave them a wobbly look, he knew exactly who he was staring at — my parents.

"Oh, Jeff. Do you remember how beautiful our wedding day was?" my mother was saying wistfully.

"Yes," my dad said with a warm smile, his chopsticks poised over his lo mein.

My mom made a face. "No you don't," she quipped back. "You fainted the moment I walked down the aisle."

My dad thought back on that fateful night for a moment. "I remember the reception," he said with certainty.

Back at the wedding, Geena was having a full-blown conversation with Nate, the waiter. They were at the bar. Geena was leaning her head on one hand and looking longingly into Nate's eyes while he filled her in on his life story.

"So I was thinking of eventually taking over my family's bakery," Nate told her as he arranged some appetizers on a platter. "You ever been to the old Cincinnati Bread Company on Cincinnati Street?"

"Did you say *Cincinnati*?" *Did* he say Cincinnati?

This is when I interrupted their romantic moment as I came frantically running from the other side of the banquet hall, arms and hair flailing the whole way.

"Geena!" I cried as I busted between her and

Nate. "I saw Jake! But . . ." I paused, picturing what had happened. "He couldn't hear me."

Nate gave me a polite smile and picked up his tray. "I've got samosas to circulate," he told Geena. "See you later?"

"Yeah," Geena said dreamily back to him. I don't think she even knew I was there. I watched Nate move away from us and then got right back to my story.

"Anyway, I just saw Patti Perez. I don't think she saw me, but . . ." Geena was still staring off after Nate and it didn't seem like she was listening to a word I said. I snapped my fingers in front of her face. "Geena, hello?" I had important stuff to talk about here!

"Sorry," Geena said with a smile, coming back to reality. "What were you saying? Something about Patti Perez?"

"Yeah. She's —" But I never got to finish my sentence.

"Here," said a smug voice from behind me. I jumped to Geena's side and felt my stomach tie itself in a knot when I saw Patti standing there. She was sneering and she had a determined look in her eyes. There was an enormous man dressed in black standing behind her with his arms crossed over his chest, looking down at us. "These are the wedding crashers I told you about," she told him. And that's all he needed to provide us with a private escort — *out* of the wedding.

Back at the tattoo parlor, Ben was looking over the tattoo options on the wall one more time before making his final decision. His eyes were fixed on a large, ropy snake wrapped around thorny roses and a banner that had room for personalized lettering. He turned to the man behind him, who had just about every part of his face pierced and tattoos all over his body, and pointed out the snake.

"Yeah. I can do that for you," said the man with a nod as he headed over to where he worked. He sat on a stool that was next to a chair that looked like it had come out of a dentist's office. Only the chair wasn't anywhere near as clean as a dentist's and I would never let this guy touch my teeth! I can't believe Ben was actually going to have this guy come at him with a needle. "What do you want the banner to say?"

Ben grabbed a pen and a piece of paper from a nearby table and scrawled something on it before handing it to the tattoo guy.

The guy looked at it and read aloud, "Jen Fever."

"Forever. It says *forever*," Ben said emphatically.

The guy looked at the paper again. Then he looked at Ben and scrunched up his face. "How old did you say you were?"

Ben looked uncomfortable. "Twenty-six," he answered.

After another skeptical look, the guy shrugged his shoulders and grabbed his tattooing tool. "Roll up your sleeve," he directed.

Ben slowly rolled up the sleeve of his T-shirt. As the needle buzzed to life and started moving toward his arm, Ben began to have second thoughts about this whole tattoo plan. He shrank back into the chair, closed his eyes tight, and pinched his face up. He had to brace himself for contact with that horrible, buzzing needle.

From that tattoo parlor somewhere in Chinatown, a loud scream pierced the night as the guy started Ben's tattoo.

I'm pretty sure all of Chinatown could hear Ben's scream.

"AAAAARRRRRRRRRGH!"

Back at the Hong Kong Palace, Zach was still hiding behind the lobster tank and listening to my parents on their date.

"Do you remember our first date here?" my mom was asking my dad.

"Yes," my dad said with a warm smile.

"No you don't. The orange chicken chilies were so hot, you passed out under the table." Jeez, Mom, give the guy a break.

"True. But . . ." He glanced around the room for a moment, as if looking for something he recognized, and then dove under the table.

"Jeff!" my mom said with a roll of her eyes. "Jeff, what are you doing?" she asked my dad's feet, which were now facing her across the table.

My dad let out a laugh. "Ha! It's still here! 'Jeff plus Sue equals love.' Ha-ha!" Chuckling, he made his way back into his seat. "I carved that under the table when I came to. I can't believe it's still there!" He thought for a second. "I couldn't have been older than Ben," he said in disbelief.

"I miss the kids. I hope they're okay." Mom, you've only been out for, like, an hour!

"I'm sure they're fine," Dad tried to reassure her.

Back at Jake's cousin's wedding, Geena and I were being unceremoniously pushed out the back door of the reception hall into the back alley. Yeah, the back alley where restaurants have their Dumpsters and leave all their trash. It was just us and the Dumpsters.

"Wow. This comes in as a close second to the time I flushed my skirt down the toilet as the most embarrassing moment of my life," Geena declared.

I turned back to the big man who had shown us out and put on my most pathetic face possible. "Wait! No! I have to get a message to someone in there," I said, trying to get myself in front of the door so that he couldn't lock us out.

"What do I look like, a carrier pigeon?" No. Actually, you couldn't look less like a pigeon. A huge, ugly vulture, maybe. But a cute pigeon? I don't think so.

"But he's leaving for Canada in the morning and if I don't tell him how I really feel, it's over." Even a huge, ugly vulture has a heart. Right?

He stopped for a moment as though he was considering how bad it might actually be for me if everything were really over. "Perfect," he spat back at me, slamming the door as he went back inside.

No. This can't be happening. I could feel one of those all-consuming screams rising up in my chest again. This night was just getting worse and worse.

"You know what? Just forget it. Let's go home." I'd had enough frustration for one night. I started walking out of the alley toward the street.

"So, Jake will spend the rest of his life with Patti Perez?" Geena prodded me as she matched my stride.

"Pretty much." Time to try to look for the silver lining. What else do people come to Chinatown for? We made the trip. We might as well get something out of it. "I wonder if they sell mogwais here. You know, the gremlins before they become gremlins. What are the rules? You can't feed them past midnight and you can't get them wet?"

"Quit talking nonsense." I guess Geena wasn't interested in tracking down cute little pre-monsters while we were here. "All we have to do is change clothes and sneak back in."

"Change into what?"

Geena and I stepped from the alley out onto the main street again. There were a bunch of stores lining the sidewalk with street-side displays. The one we were standing in front of was selling large pieces of brightly colored fabric that I think most people would have bought to make into drapes. Geena looked at the cloth hanging on display for a moment and then a look crossed her face. I know that look. It's a look that says, *I just figured out exactly how we're going to solve all our problems.* But she was looking at fabric.

"We're going to disguise ourselves as curtains?" I asked her uncertainly. I really wasn't understanding how home decor was going to get us out of this situation.

Back at the restaurant, Zach was crouched behind the lobster tank, getting ready to make his move. My parents were still reminiscing.

"Where did the time go?" my dad wondered wistfully.

"Time flies when you're passed out for most of it." My mom can be pretty funny when she wants to be.

"I can't believe it's been *nineteen* years. Nineteen wonderful years." I think my dad was trying to get my mom's mind off of all the times he'd passed out and back onto how great their time together had been. But I think if my husband had passed out at every major event of our relationship, I'd probably think about it a lot, too.

As a waiter passed between Zach and the table where my parents sat, the time finally came for him to move to the next phase of his rescue mission. Zach grabbed a dumpling off the waiter's tray and, with a long arched gesture, tossed it onto the table in front of my dad. I guess Zach's basketball skills are useful in real life after all. A lot of people would have found a dumpling landing on their table out of nowhere strange, but my dad's never given free food a second thought.

"This must be some kind of free sample," my dad said, picking the dumpling up in his chopsticks and looking around for its origin. He raised the dumpling as if he were making a toast and said, "Compliments of the chef!" as he popped the whole thing into his mouth.

While my dad was enthralled with his dumpling, Zach jumped behind the next waiter that passed by and started to walk in sync with him across the restaurant to find a place to sit. Careful to keep the waiter between him and my parents at all times, Zach stealthily matched his steps to the waiter's until he reached an empty booth. He jumped into the booth and grabbed a menu, opening it up and holding it in front of him to shield himself from my parents' view. Now he was ready to get that lobster out of the tank and out of this restaurant. All he needed to do was order it for his dinner.

But that was when he heard the voices of the couple next to him as they decided what to order.

"Are you in the mood for lobster? Because I sure am," the short, balding, tubby man in the next booth said in a loud, chortling voice.

The slim blond woman across from him looked impressed. "Oooh. Lobster sounds great."

The man looked over to the tank where Zach's lobster was wandering around and looking lonely. "Oh, but there's only one left," the man said, looking sympathetic for a moment before he laughed ghoulishly and leaned toward the woman, saying loudly, "Too bad for you! *Garçon!*" he called, looking around the room for a waiter and snapping his fingers in the air.

The woman eyed the little balding man irritably. It's hard to understand how an attractive woman like that would end up with such an annoying guy. She considered him for another moment as he kept searching for a waiter and said, "You know, you looked much taller in your i-match photo."

"I know!" the man cackled, still looking around. "*Garçon!* Come on!"

Zach's eyes were wide with fear as he heard the couple discussing their dinner. He would have to act fast if he was going to save that lobster from ending up as the obnoxious man's feast. He grabbed the next waiter that walked within reach of him and quickly said, "I'll have the lobster."

The waiter looked impressed by Zach's sophisticated — and expensive — choice. "Excellent. With drawn butter?"

Zach's eyes got even bigger. I guess he forgot that most restaurants cook the food before they bring it to you. "Ah! No! Alive."

"Oh," the waiter responded. But then Zach's request kind of sank in and he gave him a questioning look. "Pardon me, sir?"

Zach was thinking so fast you could almost see the parts of his brain working. "It's the new diet craze," he declared enthusiastically. "Live is the new raw."

"Yes, sir." The waiter looked skeptical. But as they say, the customer is always right. "Right away, sir." And he headed off to get Zach's order together. As he passed my mom and dad's table, my dad took the opportunity to thank the restaurant for his complimentary airborne appetizer.

"Thank you for the dumpling," my dad said to the waiter. "It was excellent."

"What?" the waiter asked, looking confused. Which is understandable, when you think about it.

My dad thought for a second and then busted out with some phrase in Chinese followed by "dumpling." I don't have any idea where my dad picked up Chinese, or rather where he *thought* he picked up Chinese, but what I think he actually said to the waiter was "Have a happy new year, dumpling."

My mom gave my dad a loving but slightly exasperated look. "Oh, Jeff. Sometimes I think you talk just to hear yourself talk."

"Really?" I guess he was considering what she said. "What do you know — I do do that, don't I? But then again," he continued, starting to look confused and maybe a little bit hurt, "since I am the one talking, I don't know if I actually . . . hear it." Poor Dad.

As you might expect, live lobster doesn't take that long to prepare. The waiter was already on his way back to Zach's carrying a plate with Zach's friend perched on top.

"Here's your lobster, sir," the waiter said cordially as he placed the plate in front of Zach. He also placed the bill on the table and added, "You can take care of this whenever you're ready."

"Thank you," Zach said, trying to maintain his air of

sophistication. "I'm sure I can . . ." He took one look at how much a lobster in Chinatown costs and his cool demeanor shattered. He looked desperately at the waiter and asked mildly, "This is in pesos?" Sure, Zach. Pesos. In Chinatown.

The waiter gave him an irritated look and eyed Zach's cruelty-free sneakers under the table. "Someone who can afford such expensive shoes can surely afford a nice lobster dinner." Not exactly bad logic. But how did this waiter know about cruelty-free sneakers? I kind of thought Zach was the only one. In any case, Zach knew he was going to have to find a way to pay the lobster's full price.

A few minutes later, Zach was at the restaurant's cashier, cooing softly to the lobster, which was tucked carefully into a Styrofoam take-out box. "Yeah. Yes," he said gently. "You okay? Okay."

You're probably wondering how he managed to pay for such an expensive rescue. Well, that was when Zach placed his cruelty-free sneakers on top of the bill, gingerly held his lobster in the carry-out container to his chest, and backed slowly out of the restaurant, careful not to draw my parents' attention as he passed their table. I never asked Zach how much he paid for those sneakers but I guess it was just about the same price as a lobster in Chinatown.

As Zach skulked out the door, my dad was just putting his most recent brilliant idea into action.

"Go ahead. Time it. I will not talk for the next nineteen minutes. One minute for every year that we've been married. Go ahead. Start now. Go."

"It happens to everyone," the tattoo guy said reassuringly to Ben as he helped him calm down by rubbing his back. Wow. A sensitive tattoo guy?

Ben took a break from breathing into a paper bag to ask, "Really?"

"Nah," the tattoo guy admitted. "Just the wimps. Do you want me to keep going or not?" Okay, I guess he wasn't that sensitive.

Ben considered this for a moment and then asked, "Do you have a belt I could bite down on?"

I kind of hoped Ben was joking, but before the tattoo guy could answer him, two big cops busted in through the door.

"All right, nobody move. You're under arrest for underage tattooing," one of the cops said, nodding meaningfully at Ben.

"I knew you weren't twenty-six!" the tattoo guy exclaimed, sounding hurt that Ben had lied to him. Maybe he was more sensitive than I thought!

"Did you report me?" Ben asked him incredulously.

"No," the second police officer cut in. "We could hear your screams down at the precinct."

Huh. Loud screams must run in the family.

Meanwhile, Geena had finished designing our disguises out of a couple of colorful drapes from the booth behind the restaurant. They weren't cheap; but I have to say that our traditional Indian outfits looked pretty convincing.

"Two perfect Indian saris. Am I a miracle worker or what?" Geena was never the modest type.

"We look great," I agreed.

Hey, I can be modest. But we really did look good!

"A little two-sided tape and the world is your fashion oyster. Come on." Never let anyone tell you that a firm knowledge of fashion won't get you anywhere in life.

Geena and I were now ready to make our second attempt to infiltrate Jake's cousin's wedding. We made our way to the front door of the reception hall and stepped off the street and into the restaurant.

I didn't even realize what a close call we had. Just moments before Geena and I were safely inside the restaurant, my mom and dad walked around the corner arm in arm. I guess they'd finished their dinner and decided to stroll along the romantic streets of Chinatown — at least, I imagine they were thinking it was romantic — while my mom waited out my dad's little homage to silence. She was keeping a careful eye on her watch.

"And . . . nineteen. You did it!" My dad made a gesture to indicate that nineteen minutes was nothing. He was capable of staying quiet for far longer than nineteen minutes and he was going to prove to my mom that he loved the sound of his silence just as much — or more than — he liked the sound of his own voice. "And you're going for more time," my mom said, translating my dad's flailing gestures. "Good. This is fun for me." Poor Mom.

Ben had a close call, too. He didn't realize it, but when the cops took him and put him in the back of the cruiser, he drove within feet of where my parents were walking. I guess my mom got a glimpse of him, though, because she ran into the street trying to get another look inside the police car. The woman has a sixth sense, I'm telling you.

"Is that Ben? In the back of a police car?" My dad started to try to figure out how to communicate his confusion to her silently but stopped when he thought he figured out that my mom was trying to trick him into speaking. He laughed silently at her attempt.

"No!" She was serious. And getting seriously sick of my dad's silent routine. "I — I'm going to give him a call. It would be nice to hear another voice."

In the back of the police cruiser, Ben's cell phone rang.

"Yo! Ben here."

"Ben! You're home!" Call forwarding is a pretty amazing little feature. Don't you think?

"Of course I'm home! Home is where the phone is, so . . . I'm home! Just making popcorn and watching *Back to the Future . . . Two*. Marty! Look out for the Indians!!!" Nice, Ben. Subtle.

My mom was reassured. I don't think parents are that familiar with the magic of modern telephone technology, so it never occurred to her that Ben would be anywhere *but* home. "Well, I just called to say I love you. Good night."

"You, too. Good night." Ben snapped his phone shut.

The police officer driving the cruiser shook his head shamefully at Ben while he looked at him in the rearview mirror. "What?" Ben said defensively. "Like you never snuck out of the house?"

"There were no Indians in *Back to the Future Two*. You're thinking of *Back to the Future Three*. The one where Marty goes back to 1885 to find Doc. *BTTF2* is the one where Marty buys the sports almanac. There are those who say that *BTTF2* and *BTTF3* are essentially one movie. Regardless, neither one can compare to the original *BTTF*. Man! That was one heck of a movie."

So the cop was a *Back to the Future* fan. That's normal.

Right?

This is where the story really starts to get interesting. Especially because it gets back to the best person involved in this whole night: me. Just kidding. But the story really does get good here. You see, Geena and I were finally back inside the wedding reception and I was getting closer every second to telling Jake how I really felt about him and rescuing him from Patti Perez.

"There," Geena said, pointing across the room. Patti was there and she had Jake cornered. It looked like she wasn't letting anyone get within ten feet of him.

We saw Nate then, too, as he made his way around the room with a fresh plate of appetizers. Geena's face lit up as he made his way over to us.

"Appetizer?" Nate asked, not recognizing us. We were in our fabulous new saris, remember?

Geena pushed her sari off her head and uncovered her face to reveal a huge smile and shining eyes. "Hey, Cincinnati," she said coyly to Nate. She was obviously crazy about this guy.

"Hey, you!" Nate seemed almost as happy to see Geena as she was to see him. He looked a little confused at first when she grabbed his arm and pulled him aside. She frantically whispered something in his ear that I couldn't hear. But when she finished, he smiled and walked away.

"What'd you say to him?" I was dying to know.

"Just watch," Geena said with confidence.

We turned to see Nate glide casually across the room toward Patti. When he was directly behind her, he turned suddenly and upset the tray of appetizers. Unfortunately for Patti, he managed to dump the food all down her back. If looks could kill, Nate would have been dead on the floor instantly. Since they don't, he was fine and Patti just stormed off to get herself cleaned up.

Have I ever told you that I have the best friends ever?

Geena was thrilled with Nate. "Cute. Cooks. And takes orders well. I think I'm in love. Well, what are you waiting for?" Geena asked, motioning me over to Jake with a nod.

I pulled my sari a little tighter around my shoulders and started walking over to Jake. I couldn't believe the moment I'd been hoping for all night was finally here. Was I ready for this? Would I really be able to tell him how I felt?

Yes. I was totally ready for this moment.

Jake looked up and saw me coming. "Addie! What are you doing here?" Does he look happy to see me? I think he looks happy to see me.

"I kind of crashed your cousin's wedding. I really need to talk to you." Okay. So far so good.

"Really? Because last time we talked, you said you

hated me." Oh, yeah. I forgot about that. But I guess it was pretty fresh in Jake's mind.

"What? No. That was just —" But I never finished explaining because these guys walked in between us and one of them told Jake he had to go take some pictures with his family.

"I gotta go," Jake said, still looking a little confused.

"Well, come find me when you're done. I'll be here." I was trying to sound chipper and relaxed. But honestly, I was totally freaking out. You have to go? But I was so close! This is *so* something that would happen to me!

Right around now was when Ben arrived at the precinct jail with the police officer. He was trying to get his movie trivia straightened out.

"So, when did Marty and Doc take Manhattan?" he asked the police officer with concern.

The cop shook his head sadly. "That was the Muppets." And with that, he slammed the door of Ben's cell closed.

A voice from behind him made Ben turn around. "Hey. Look who's here."

A satisfied look crossed Ben's face as he approached the person sitting on the bench behind him in the cell. "I didn't know they could arrest a guy for being a jerk, Jerk." In case you're still wondering, it was Kirk. Ben can be so witty sometimes.

I'm not sure this was one of those times, though. I mean, he did think there were Muppets in *Back to the Future.*

"Ha," Kirk said, not really sounding that amused. "They brought me in for the acrobat brawl. Guess I'm not the only one who fled from the law, huh?" Kirk figured two could play at this criminal-record game.

"Oh, yeah. That was a fun fight. We should do it again sometime." Ben started to take off his button-down shirt as he approached Kirk. Kirk stood up from the bench and moved menacingly toward Ben, looking unintimidated.

"How 'bout now?" Kirk suggested, getting in Ben's face.

"Gladly," Ben said as he tossed down his shirt — don't worry, he had a T-shirt on under that one — and gave Kirk a shove in the chest with both hands. Kirk shoved him back. Ben shoved Kirk again. Yeah, this was a pretty crazy fight.

But it was over a second later when Kirk tried to grab Ben by the tops of his arms. As soon as he touched the spot where Ben had gotten his tattoo, which was covered by the T-shirt he was wearing, Ben winced and cried out in pain as he backed away.

"Ow! My tattoo!" Ben cried as he covered the spot protectively with his hand.

"A tattoo?" Kirk asked in disbelief. "Aren't you like — twelve?" Now he was laughing. Bearing witness to Ben's attempt to "grow up" was clearly entertaining to him.

"Sixteen!" Ben declared. Kirk just laughed more. "Yeah. I did the crime," Ben said in his best rebel voice. "And now — I'm gonna do the time." Ben shrugged his shoulders in a tough-guy motion. "That's how much I care about Jen. I'll endure any amount of pain to win her back." And with that, Ben lifted the sleeve of his T-shirt to show Kirk just how grown-up and how crazy about Jen he was by revealing his tattoo.

At least, I *think* it was a tattoo. Honestly, it looked more like an ink stain. Or maybe a bruise like you get when someone gives you a Smurf bite. You know, those really painful little pinches? Whatever it was, it wasn't exactly screaming, "Supermature and macho guy here!"

"You call *that* a tattoo?" Kirk was still laughing. "*This* is a tattoo."

Kirk ripped apart the buttons at the top of his shirt, pulled it open, and revealed his chest — where there was a full picture of a yacht complete with sails, oars, and crew members scattered around the deck. Yeah, I think Kirk had the mature and macho act down a *little* bit better than Ben.

Ben looked down at his own mini-tattoo and then back at Kirk's chest. He looked back and forth a couple of times, kind of taking the whole thing in. Then he rushed over to the bars of his cell, stuck his head out as much as he could, and called to whoever could hear him, "Could I get my one call now?"

Jake had gone over to stand with his family on some stairs while a man with a camera took photo after photo of them all just standing there. He never even moved them around or changed the combinations of people or anything.

"Come on! You already took that photo! Ten times!" I didn't say this loud enough for anyone to hear but, I mean, come on! How many copies of *Wedding Party on the Stairs* did they need to take? I was all ready to talk to Jake and waiting around was killing me.

My phone rang. When I pulled it out and looked at the caller ID, I saw that it was Ben. Why could he possibly be calling? He had to have tracked down Jen by now.

"What do you want?" I tried to be clear with my voice that I was *not* happy about being interrupted.

"I'm in jail. I need you to bail me out." Jail? Did Ben really just tell me that he's in *jail*?

"What?" You're probably thinking the same thing I was right then: *There goes my perfect moment with Jake.* I couldn't answer him, I was so mad.

"Addie?"

I kept thinking and not answering. Maybe I shouldn't go. Maybe I should just let Ben rot in jail.

"Addie?"

In my head I pictured what I wanted to do: "Enjoy the slammer. I'll visit you for Hanukkah." I slammed the phone shut and dashed to the stairs where Jake was standing with his family. Madly pushing anyone who stood between me and Jake out of my way — including his mother and a couple of grandparents, who went toppling off the stairs — I cleared a path through the crowd. When I got to Jake, I grabbed him by the collar and shook him just so he'd know how serious I was.

"I like you! I really like you!" I yelled at him.

"Addie!" Jake cried in confused dismay, looking at the family members I'd tossed aside to get to him.

Too much?

"Addie?" Ben asked again. Yeah. In *real* life, which is not a perfect world in case you didn't know that already, I was still on the phone with Ben. My brother, Ben, who was in jail. I sighed, knowing what I had to do.

"I'm coming." I hung up the phone, gave one last look at Jake on the stairs, and went to get Geena so we could go bail my brother out of jail.

I can't believe I have to go bail my *brother* out of *jail*! Is this really my life? I think I must be about the best sister in the whole entire world.

Stupid brother.

On our way out of the wedding, Geena and I were reunited with Zach, who'd made his way from the Hong Kong Palace to the place where the wedding reception was being held. Did I mention that Zach wasn't alone? He was with his lobster.

"So? Did you tell him? What happened?" Zach asked when he saw us. Then he seemed to take a better look at us. "Why are you guys wearing curtains?" Jeez, Zach, if you were so interested you could have come to help me instead of running off to save a lobster.

"Do you have any money?" I asked. I wasn't in the mood to get him caught up on everything, and this night was ending up being a bigger drain on my wallet than I had expected.

"None. I even had to give up my sneakers to pay for Dolores."

"Dolores?" Geena and I were both confused.

Zach took the lobster out of its take-out container and held her up by way of introduction. "It's Spanish for 'pain.'" Cute. "But why do we need money, anyway?"

"My idiot brother landed himself in jail. We spent all *our* money on these curtains — sorry, I mean *saris*."

"Hey, guys! What are you doing here?" It was Duane. And he was with Mary Ferry. I was saved!

"Do you guys have any money?" I asked desperately.

"I always keep emergency cash in my bra," Mary said proudly.

Duane gave Mary a funny look. "You do?"

Mary nodded proudly. "Shield me," she instructed me and Geena. If there was ever a good use for curtains that you happen to be wearing as a sari in order to sneak into a wedding, shielding a friend so she can remove her emergency money from her bra is it. Geena and I moved into a doorway with Mary and lifted the edge of our curtains up over our heads. Mary wouldn't have been more out of view in her own private dressing room.

A moment later, after a little shifting and rustling

behind the screen Geena and I were providing, Mary's hand shot above the curtain, holding her cash.

Zach and Duane, who had been looking confused a moment before, were totally impressed.

"I love her!" Duane told Zach proudly.

I was totally loving her right then, too! I took the money from her hand as I gushed my thanks. "Thank you so much, Mary! I promise I'll pay you back!" And then I realized how much money I was actually holding.

Twenty dollars.

"Twenty dollars?" I guess Mary's emergencies weren't supposed to include things like bailing people out of jail, which I'm pretty sure costs more than twenty dollars. "This isn't enough. We have to think of something. Fast."

Geena thought for a second and then said, "I have an idea! It's not exactly fast but . . ."

But nothing! At this point, I'd take any idea I could get!

And that's how we ended up back in the alley with the turtle racers.

"This is Jet Li," said the first man, pointing to the turtle with the number one painted on his shell.

"And this," the man next to him continued, pointing at the turtle with the number two painted on his shell, "is Bruce Lee. No relation," he clarified, gesturing between the two turtles.

Geena's big idea? It was to grow our twenty dollars into more — by betting it on a turtle race.

Here goes nothing.

"Okay. We'll put twenty dollars on . . ." I looked between the two to try to pick the winner. But I just couldn't decide. I mean, they were both turtles. Should I pick the one with the longer legs? The one with the lighter-looking shell? I resorted to a round of eenie-meenie-miny-moe to try to settle this once and for all.

"That one," I said, pointing to turtle number one.

"Good pick," said the man who, I guess, trained Jet Li. "Since you kissed him, Jet Li hasn't lost a race." That was promising. "A win with him pays two to one."

Two to one? Let's see . . . that means if I put down twenty and get twice as much back I'll win . . . forty dollars?

"I don't think forty dollars is going to be enough," Geena said, shaking her head.

She was right. "We'll be here all night," I agreed.

Then Zach cut into the bargaining with a sly look on his face. "What if we raise the stakes a little higher?" He started to open his take-out container and held up his lobster for everyone to see. "How much do we win if Dolores beats the turtles?"

The men all started laughing and knocking one other on the arm when they saw Dolores.

"A lobster," said Jet Li's owner between chortles. "That's rich!"

"Especially when boiled and dipped in hot butter!" Bruce Lee's owner laughed back at him.

Zach was taken aback at the mention of consuming his new friend and put Dolores protectively back into her take-out box.

"Well," Jet Li's owner said, looking thoughtful. "I don't like to take money from children . . . but if you guys win, we'll pay you ten-to-one odds." Ten to one?

"If Dolores wins, Mary Ferry's bra money turns into two hundred dollars!" Geena was fast with math when it came to money.

"But if *we* win," Jet Li's owner continued, "lobster dinner tonight!" The men were rubbing their hands together and looking excited at the prospect of a cheap lobster landing right in their laps. Zach looked a lot more worried now and clutched the Styrofoam container to his chest.

But Geena was in control of this bargain. "You're on!" she said to the men.

Zach reluctantly started to move Dolores from her container to a lane on the track but Geena stopped him.

"Addie? Do you want to kiss her?" she asked me. Well, if it worked for Jet Li . . .

The race was one of those moments that's really hard to describe. It involved three of the slowest animals on Earth ambling from one end of a wooden racetrack to the other while three kids and a bunch of Chinese men surrounding them jumped up and down yelling, screaming, and hollering for the animals to go faster, even though it was pretty clear that the animals had no interest or even the ability to go any faster.

All three animals seemed neck and neck to me. Wait, do lobsters even have necks? Whatever. It was really close. But then, suddenly, it was as though Dolores realized what was at stake and put on a burst of speed. Well, maybe *burst* and *speed* aren't really the right words to describe what happened. But whatever it was, suddenly Dolores was clearly out in front.

"Win, darn you, Jet Li!" one of the turtle men yelled desperately as turtle number one fell noticeably behind the lobster.

And then, wouldn't you know it? Dolores crossed that finish line way ahead of the turtles.

"I knew you could do it, Dolores!" Zach was like a proud father with his winning lobster. He hugged Dolores to his chest, gushing with praise for her. "Oh, I love you, you crazy lobster!" Then his look of love turned suddenly to one of distress. "Ow. PAIN! Oh, pain! Pain!" Zach moved his hands to the side and we realized that now Dolores was being held to Zach's chest by her claws, which had clamped down through his shirt on his skin.

Looks like that lobster was well named.

Back in jail, Ben was having something of an epiphany.

"I guess my tattoo wouldn't have impressed her that much after all," he said sadly as he looked from his ink stain to Kirk's yacht.

Kirk got a funny look on his face then as he started to talk about Jen. "She's not impressed by normal things.

I mean, that's what's so great about her. It's so cute how she flips her hair back, all sassy." Wow. He was head over heels for that girl.

"Really?" Ben asked, picturing in his mind Jen flipping her hair. "I always thought it was kind of annoying."

"Oh! And her laugh?" Kirk was in la-la land.

"Like nails on a chalkboard. Right?" Ben asked.

Kirk pulled himself out of his reverie and gave Ben a funny look. "What *did* you like about her?"

Ben thought for a moment before coming up with: "I liked that she liked me." Nice, Ben. But I think he was kind of catching on to something about Kirk and Jen now. "I liked a lot of things about her. Just . . . not as many as you."

"She's the perfect girl," Kirk said with a glassy-eyed look.

"It's really great that you think that," Ben said warmly as he took a seat next to Kirk on the bench. "You guys make a great couple." Huh. Looks like Ben was really doing some growing up tonight after all.

Kirk seemed happy that the two of them were finally seeing eye to eye. "Oh, you," Kirk said as he gave Ben a playful punch in the arm.

"Ow!" Ben said, flinching in pain. Kirk just couldn't

stop touching Ben's "tattoo." But at least Ben tried to look friendly while he did it.

That's when I walked in with the police officer and identified my convict brother.

"That's him," I said, pointing him out.

"Addie!" Ben jumped up and came to the door of the cell. I don't know if I've ever seen Ben look so happy to see me.

"I paid your bail. You're all good." I mentioned that I'm the best sister ever, right?

"Thank you so much! I owe you forever. Why are you wearing curtains?" Everyone seems to fixate on the curtains.

"I don't want to talk about it," I said, expecting Ben to press me on the issue. But apparently he didn't really care, anyway.

"Good. Because I need you to do something for me." Oh. Right. Bailing him out wasn't enough? "Do you have any money left?" Ben asked as he gestured to Kirk, who was now sitting alone in the cell with a forlorn look on his face.

I gave Ben my best "you've got to be kidding me" look. But actually, Dolores's win paid enough that I *did* have some money left over.

Once we'd gotten Kirk's bail straightened away, the five of us headed out of the jail and hit the street, just in time to see Jen running up with a wad of cash in her hand.

"I got the bail money!" Jen said as she ran up to the door of the jail. Then she realized with confusion that Kirk wasn't actually in jail anymore. "You're already out?"

"Yeah," Kirk said with a smile as he put his arm around Ben's shoulder and managed one more time to touch Ben's tattoo. "Ben bailed me out."

Jen gave Ben a curious look. "Really? That was so . . ."

"Mature?" Ben said, standing up a little straighter and looking proud of himself.

"Yeah. Ben, listen . . ." This was the first time in a while that Jen had looked at Ben with anything more than annoyance, and I have to say that Ben impressed me by what he did next.

"Can't talk. Addie's got a wedding to go to." Ben put his fingers in his mouth and made a loud whistle. A second later, seemingly from out of nowhere —

"What's up, friend? Ricky Rickshaw at your service." Ricky pulled up next to where we were standing.

I think the big tip Ben gave Ricky earlier in the evening was paying off.

"Get in. I'll meet you guys at the car," Ben said as he gestured to the seats in the carriage.

It was great that we had the chance to get back to the wedding, but then I realized something.

"We're all out of money," I pointed out. Bailing two people out of jail was pretty much all Dolores's winnings could cover. There wasn't even enough left over for a ride in a rickshaw.

"No money *and* no sneakers," Zach added, pointing to his shoeless feet.

"Nah! Ricky Rickshaw's got your back. Your brother gave me such a fat tip earlier that I went and gorged myself on some lobster. *Mmmm.*" Zach looked bothered by this, but I didn't have the energy to console him. "Ricky Rickshaw could use the exercise."

"Addie? I don't think this is so safe for Dolores." Give me a break, Zach. It's not like Ricky had a pot of boiling water in his rickshaw and, despite the earlier declaration, I don't think the *live food* movement was so popular that Dolores was in any real danger. I just gave him a look and pushed him into the carriage. We were going to that wedding.

And it's a good thing we did. Because right after we pulled away from the curb, my mom and dad wandered by. Mom was eating an ice cream.

"This is so great. You should try it." My mom looked hopefully at my dad but he just shook his head. I guess he was still not talking. "Oh, please, Jeff. For the love of all that is good, talk!"

He looked defiant. "Why? So I can hear myself talk?"

"I love when you try to talk Chinese." My mom was really exasperated now. "And when you faint at the drop of a hat. I mean, those are the things that make you *you*. Those are the reasons why I have loved you for nineteen years." She glanced up just then, which happened to be just when Ricky was pulling us past where they were walking.

"Hey. Was that Addie being pulled in a rickshaw with Geena and Zach?" She was staring after the rickshaw only half believing that it could have been us. Fortunately, my dad didn't think it was possible. I mean, we were all at home watching a movie, right? Hadn't my mom just called home a little while ago and talked to Ben?

"Okay. Why don't we get you home? Hmm?" He put his arm comfortingly around her shoulders. Good old

Dad. He thought my mom losing it was more likely than the three of us riding by in a rickshaw. "Yeah. It's been a long night. A *long* night."

We pulled up in front of the banquet hall just as the last few guests were walking out the door. It looked like the reception was over.

"Dang!" Ricky declared. "I was hoping to get some post-wedding fares. But it looks like everybody's gone."

"No!" I cried. Not *everyone* could be gone. We jumped out of the rickshaw and ran for the door. Zach held it open for me and Geena as we rushed into the banquet hall.

But the only people there were the staff. They were vacuuming and cleaning up all the decorations. All of the guests were gone.

"No. No. No, no, no!" I looked around desperately. There had to be some people still here! How can everyone be gone? This can't be my life!

"Geena!" Oh, yeah. Remember Nate? He was part of the staff and so he was still there. "I thought you left."

"I did," Geena said with a sigh. "Apparently so did everyone else."

"Yeah. The party's over," Nate said casually, like it was no big deal that everyone was gone. "But I saved a tray of cake in the back if you want to hang out." Oh, great. Cake.

Geena looked at me with concern. "I don't know. I . . ."

"Go ahead." I didn't need everyone to miss their chance at love just because I did. "My life's over, anyway."

"Great! Thanks." And with that, I watched as Geena headed off to the kitchen. I know she would have given him up and stayed with me if I'd asked her to, but there really wasn't any reason *both* of our nights needed to end badly. Geena had done so much already, she deserved to have some cake with Nate.

"Well, you can't say you didn't try," Zach tried to console me. "Do you need a hug?" But he stopped and cocked his head to one side before he could hug me. "Do you hear bells?"

"Bells? The fortune-teller said, 'The bells will lead you to your heart's desire.' I listened. And I heard bells! Little tinkling bells. They were really faint and sounded like they were coming from the back of the building. I had nothing to lose at this point, so I might as well see what the fortune-teller was talking about. After all, she had been right about Cincinnati.

I followed the sound of the bells as it got a little bit louder and a little bit louder. It was definitely coming from the back of the building. It turned out I was following the same path we'd been shown the first time we were escorted out of the party. The next thing I knew, I had followed the sound out the back door and into the alley where all the Dumpsters were. But I could still hear those bells.

I listened for another moment and then followed the sound over to one of the Dumpsters. Sure enough, when I looked inside, there was a cell phone. It was partly buried in garbage and it was ringing.

"The trash. Perfect." But I'd come this far, right? So I leaned over as far as I could, trying to reach that phone, which was, of course, just out of my reach in a really deep Dumpster. I reached a little farther and then . . . I fell into the trash headfirst. Isn't it amazing how this stuff keeps happening to me?

But at least I had the phone in hand. I might as well answer it.

"Hello?"

"Addie?" asked a voice that I definitely recognized.

"Jake?" It was Jake! I was talking to Jake!

"What are you doing in the Dumpster?" Wait. How did he know I was in the Dumpster? I looked around and there he was, standing in the alley looking at me. Yup. I had looked great in two different outfits tonight and when do I finally get Jake alone? When I'm covered in trash. Fabulous.

"Oh. Well. This phone started ringing and . . ." How was I going to explain this exactly? Fortunately, I didn't really have to.

"It's mine," Jake said. "It got lost at the reception." Remember Patti dropping Jake's phone in the trash? "I called from my mom's phone to see if I could find it. But I, uh, guess I found you, too." Did he look happy? I think he looks happy! "What are you doing here, anyway?"

Okay. Here goes. "I came here to tell you something. Jake, I like you. A lot." That wasn't so hard. Now keep going. "I mean, if you still like me, which I don't think you do since you came here with Patti . . . and I totally crashed this wedding like an idiot, but —"

"Addie." Jake stopped me and gave me a funny look. He reached over and pulled something out of my hair. "You have curry vindaloo in your hair." Oh. Great.

"This was a terrible idea," I said out loud. Would Jake really like someone he found in a Dumpster with curry vindaloo in her hair? I don't even know what that is, but I'm pretty sure most people don't put it in their hair.

"I like curry vindaloo. And . . . I like you, too." He likes me? Jakes likes me? "And I never liked Patti. Her family got invited to the wedding. I've been trying to avoid her all weekend."

Jake likes me! And he doesn't like Patti! My head was spinning — could this moment really be happening? Quick, say something back to him!

"Me, too, actually." I smiled awkwardly. Okay. Not great. But who cares? He likes me!

"I can't believe you came all the way out to Chinatown. Was it hard finding the place?"

"You have no idea." But it was totally worth every turtle-racing, curtain-wearing, jail-bailing moment!

"I'm glad you did."

And you are not going to believe what happened next. We were standing there in the alley looking at each other and, the next thing I knew, Jake was moving a little closer to me. And I was moving a little closer to him. It was like there was this strange force moving our faces closer and closer together. I could feel butterflies going crazy in my stomach as, suddenly, Jake was inches from my face. I closed my eyes and the most amazing thing in the world happened.

He kissed me!

Yes. Standing right there, Jake Behari actually kissed me. I swear fireworks went off somewhere in Chinatown at exactly that moment because there were bright lights and I'm pretty sure the earth shook a little bit.

"Perfect."

"What did you say?" Oh. Had I said that out loud?

I took the whole scene in again. Jake and me in a back alley surrounded by Dumpsters, with me in a curtain and trash in my hair. But you know what? I didn't care about any of that.

"I said, perfect."

Jake smiled. "Yeah." Then his phone rang again. He looked down at the caller ID. "I have to go. But can I call you? And e-mail you and IM you?"

Was he kidding?

"Yes, yes . . . and yes." And then, with one more amazing smile, Jake took off.

While the most fabulous thing to ever happen to me in my entire life was going on (did I mention that Jake Behari *kissed* me?), Ben made his way back to where we'd left the car to cool off. Jen was waiting by the car when he got there.

"Hey," she said with a smile.

"Hey." Ben looked quizzical. "What are you doing here?"

"I thought I could drive you home." I wonder how she knew about Ben's problems getting us here. "To thank you for bailing out Kirk."

"No, thanks," Ben said, shaking his head. "It's time I start shifting gears." I know Ben was talking about the car, but I kind of think he might have meant more than that, too.

I think Jen even looked at him with affection at that point. "If anyone can do it, you can, Knieval."

"Thanks, trainee." That's when Jen gave Ben a friendly squeeze on the arm — right where he'd been tattooed. "Ow!"

"What is it?" Jen asked with concern.

"Nothing." Ben shook his head and looked kind of . . . I don't know . . . wise. "Trust me. It's nothing."

Zach, Geena, and I walked up just as Jen was about to leave. She took one look at us and started laughing.

"What are you laughing at?" I asked her.

"A guy in socks carrying a lobster and two girls in curtains," Jen answered, still laughing and gesturing at each of us in turn. She walked away, still chuckling to herself.

"I told you Chinatown's full of strange people," Ben said with a raised eyebrow as he opened the back door of the car for Zach and Geena.

Geena jumped right back into her role of driving instructor. "Okay, now, slowly let up on the clutch, and ease down on the gas."

Ben just smiled at her, looking totally relaxed. "It's okay. I've got it."

The car ride home was as smooth as could be. I don't know how Ben was suddenly able to drive a stick. What I do know was that for all four of us — Zach with Dolores in his lap, Geena thinking about the next time she'd see Nate, Ben knowing he was over Jen, and I don't think I even have to tell you what I was thinking about — that was probably one of the best car rides ever.

Before we knew it, we were home but it was only minutes before my parents were supposed to walk through the door. Zach, Geena, and I took our places on the couch and Ben grabbed the spot in the easy chair. We tried to look as casual as possible.

Then Geena noticed that Zach was taking Dolores out of her take-out container and putting her on the coffee table.

"What are you doing?" she asked with a note of disgust.

"She needs to stretch her legs. If she stays in the box too long after that race, she'll cramp up." Once Dolores had been given room to roam, Zach started shoveling popcorn hungrily into his mouth. In his fervor to rescue Dolores and with all the excitement of the race, he hadn't actually eaten anything all night and he was ready to make up for lost meals.

"In case they ask," Ben prepped us, "we watched *Back to the Future Two*. There aren't any Muppets. The Muppets are actually in Manhattan. . . ."

"Hey, kids. We're home!" my mom called cheerfully as she and my dad walked into the house.

"Hey!" Geena and I said. We noticed we still had our purses in our hands so we simultaneously tossed them over our shoulders to the other side of the room.

"Happy anniversary!" Geena said cheerfully.

"Mnphy munifuthury, nithter and nithith Eth," Zach said through his mouth full of popcorn.

My mom made her way into the living room, looking happy from her night on the town. Then she stopped and kind of cocked her head to one side as she looked at the coffee table.

"Is that a lobster on the table?" *Oops.*

My dad, who hadn't made his way into the living room yet, still thought my mom was hallucinating. "This is getting ridiculous. You've been seeing things all night. Frankly? I'm getting a little worried about —" But my mom picked the lobster up off the table and held it up for my dad to see. He took one look at it and his eyes kind of rolled up into his head. Then he passed out and fell to the floor in a heap.

"And now our anniversary is complete," my mom declared, looking at my father on the floor. It would have been nice if my fainting father would distract her from the questions that would surely come from Dolores. No such luck.

"Now. About this lobster."

I smiled as innocently as I could. "Would you buy anniversary present?" From the expression on my mom's face, I understood what she was thinking. "Okay. Maybe not."

So now Ben and I are spending most of our days in the storeroom of Singer Sporting Goods. My dad decided the best way for us to make up for our totally forbidden journey into Chinatown was to do grunt work at the store. Ben was pretty upset, but my life was so good overall that there was no way even being in a basement all day putting shoe boxes on shelves was going to bring me down.

"This is worse than jail," Ben grumbled as he handed me some shoe boxes.

"Uh-huh." *Jake Behari.*

"I'm never driving Mom's car. I am never going to Chinatown. And I am *never* getting a tattoo again."

"Uh-huh." *Jake Behari* likes *me.*

"Think Dad's going to make us work down here all summer?"

"Uh-huh." *Jake Behari* kissed me.

"What are *you* so happy about?"

"Uh-huh." *Does life get better than this? Wait, is Ben asking me something?* "Oh. Sorry. Were you talking to me?" Ben just shook his head and went back to work.

The rest of the summer went by so quickly. Jake and I talked on the phone and IMed all the time. Sometimes we would talk for hours or write really long notes to each other. And sometimes, he'd just text me one single word: *Perfect.*

In fact, that word and my night finding Jake inspired me to write one of my best songs ever.

> *It wasn't perfect,*
> *But I wouldn't change it at all.*
> *In a phony sari*
> *Just to kiss that Jake Behari,*
> *But I wouldn't change it at all.*
> *I had to hike through Chinatown,*
> *Had to bail out Ben,*
> *Kissed a lobster, but I'd do it again.*
> *It wasn't pretty.*
> *It wasn't perfect.*
> *But I wouldn't change it at all.*